Halitor the Hero

By Rebecca M. Douglass

This is a work of fiction. All the characters, organizations, events and places portrayed in this novel are either products of the author's imagination or are used fictitiously.

Copyright © 2014 Rebecca M. Douglass
Cover images and design by Danielle English
http://www.kanizo.co.uk

ISBN: 1502738597
ISBN-13: 978-1502738592

DEDICATION

This book is dedicated to every kid who has asked me when I'm writing the next one. Here it is.

Children's books by Rebecca M. Douglass

The Ninja Librarian
Return to Skunk Corners (Ninja Librarian Book 2)
A is for Alpine: An Alphabet Book for Little Hikers (with
Dave Dempsey)

Adult Mystery Fiction:
Death By Ice Cream

www.ninjalibrarian.com

ACKNOWLEDGEMENTS

For my first venture into fantasy, I feel as though I ought to start by thanking C.S. Lewis and J.R.R. Tolkien, whose books started me on a love of other worlds. But then I think of so many other writers whose work I have loved over the years, and I would need to thank them all…so here it is: thank you to all the amazing writers who have come before me and whose works have shaped me as a writer and a person.

Many thanks to my library buddies who have supported me in all my writing, reading early drafts and helping to get cover designs just right. Special thanks are due to Sue Von Hagel for suggestions about the cover, and to Laurie Giusti for not only reading early drafts and helping to develop the cover, but for her excellent proofreading skills (any remaining errors are completely my own). I owe thanks and admiration to Danielle English for the beautiful cover she produced, the best yet!

My beta-reading team this time also included Lisa Frieden, Marcy Sheiner, and Jemima Pett. Thank you for your insights, which helped make this a much better book. I want to give a special thanks to Lila Magbilang, who helped me see the story as a kid sees it. Thanks for giving up some of your summer vacation to help out, Lila!

And, as always, thanks to my husband Dave and our boys, who put up with my strange writing habit.

CHAPTER ONE: HALITOR THE HAPLESS

Halitor's career as an apprentice Hero ended with a girl's scream.

The cry echoed through the woods of Loria where the young Hero and his apprentice-master rode, looking for trouble and hoping not to find it. The two riders turned toward the sound, drawn by duty to somebody's doom.

As they neared the source of the disturbance, Bovrell the Bold waved Halitor forward, and the boy spurred his horse toward the screams. His sweating hands could scarcely hold the reins as his Master shouted instructions. Halitor burst into a clearing and reined to a halt so abrupt that he nearly flew out of the saddle.

A girl with dark hair and a torn gown struggled in the grip of an ogre, and it was Halitor's job to set matters right. Under his breath Halitor muttered, "I am a Hero. I am a Hero," over and over in hopes of convincing himself it was true. He thought of the *Hero's Guide* in his saddlebag. He'd memorized the section on fighting ogres, but it didn't seem helpful now.

As Halitor prepared to dismount, the monster turned its attention to him. When it did, it loosed its grip on the Fair Maiden, who pulled herself from the ogre's grasp. Instead of running, she stood watching her rescuers. Fair Maidens, Halitor knew, were so often too frozen with fear to escape when they might.

"That's right," Bovrell the Bold called from where he sat on his horse, well away from the fight and ready to fly back down the mountain if necessary. "Fight monsters afoot, lest your horse spook and spill you."

Halitor, distracted by his apprentice-master in the act of dismounting, landed with his legs tangled. He wobbled, nearly fell, and dropped his sword, clutching at his saddle to save himself. The ogre stepped toward him with an evil grin. Before Halitor could right himself, the Fair Maiden caught up the fallen sword, turned, and stabbed the monster between the plates of its armor. Green blood poured out and the ogre fell, twitching and thrashing as it died. The girl jumped back, looking rather green herself. She turned her back on the corpse and let the sword fall, swaying. Behind her, the ogre gave a final twitch, and the clanking of armor died away as the monster stopped breathing. Bovrell rode up and jabbed the ogre once with his lance.

"'Halitor the Hero,'" Bovrell hissed as he passed the still-staggering young man. "Halitor the Hopeless. You couldn't rescue a lost kitten, let alone a Fair Maiden."

Especially not a Fair Maiden. Halitor knew that. When he got within a spear's throw of a comely maiden—and to him, from his safe distance, they were all comely—he turned more hopelessly hapless than ever. Twice in the last month Bovrell had been obliged to ride to the rescue of both Halitor and the maidens he'd been trying to save. He would never become a Hero at this rate. And now the girl he was meant to rescue had taken his sword and killed the ogre herself.

He didn't know if her action left him envious, admiring, or even more humiliated. It didn't matter. He couldn't thank or blame her, because he couldn't even open his mouth. Girls had that effect on him. They scared him, leaving him even more clumsy and tongue-tied than usual.

While Halitor stood speechless and miserable, Bovrell caught up his horse, led it to the Fair Maiden, and helped her to mount. Then both rode off.

Alone with the dead ogre, Halitor pulled off his helmet and watched them go. Desperately trying not to cry, he picked up his sword and wiped it on the grass, taking care not to look at the corpse, he sheathed the weapon and began the long walk back to their lodgings in Carthor. The late-afternoon sun beat on him until he dripped sweat, before at last it sank below the horizon. Halitor muttered and kicked at rocks as he walked. Bovrell was right. He was a thrice-cursed misbegotten fool who'd never make anything of himself. He'd been an apprentice, bound to Bovrell the Bold, for almost three years, and he would never, ever, be any good at Heroing.

Bovrell never fell over his own sword or let his horse wander off while he slept. And never, not once, had he failed in a quest because he couldn't find a clean pocket-handkerchief. Bovrell always had well-combed hair and a smooth-shaved face. Halitor's mouse-brown hair grew in several directions at once, and while he didn't yet need to shave, he kept getting pimples in unfortunate places.

All the way to their inn, and it was a long walk, Halitor muttered and grumbled and called himself seven kinds of idiot. Then he started making excuses. It wasn't his fault girls made him so nervous. She should have had more patience. He'd have picked up his sword and done the job, given enough time. Why couldn't she have waited, like a proper Fair Maiden? *The Hero's Guide to Battles, Rescues, and the Slaying of Monsters* never said anything about Fair Maidens using swords or defending themselves. To Halitor, the Guide was Truth, and he didn't know what to do about a girl who didn't follow the rules. It didn't say anything about leaving apprentices to walk home, either.

By the time he reached the Drunken Bard, the inn where he stayed with Bovrell, Halitor had decided one thing. He would have to give up the Hero business and take up a line of work where you never saw girls. Yeti-herding on the snow-covered slopes of the Ice Castle sprang to mind.

Bovrell seemed to agree that Halitor needed another line of work. When Halitor, foot-weary and heart-sore, knocked on his master's door in the small hours to tell him he was back, the Hero opened the door a crack, stuck his head out, and said, "The gods themselves couldn't teach you to be a Hero. You're sacked." Then he shut the door again.

Halitor wanted to ride out right then and prove him wrong. But he couldn't. For one thing, Bovrell wasn't wrong. Halitor knew he made a terrible hero. For another, he was too tired and hungry. So he went downstairs and found a loaf of bread in the kitchen, ate it, and went to bed.

The rising sun woke the hapless would-be Hero, though he would have preferred to sleep. He made his way to Bovrell's room, scuffling his feet and feeling sorry for himself. When he knocked on the door, no one answered. He opened it cautiously and looked in. The bed was empty. So was the corner where Bovrell had dumped his packs. Halitor turned to go to the stable and find his horse, but a rough hand descended on his bony shoulder.

"Here, boy! Your master's gone off without paying, but I'll have it out of you, by Scarpeg!"

Halitor turned. "I can't pay, sir. He took everything. He didn't even give me my pocket-money." He swallowed hard to keep from crying. "He said I was sacked, because I'm a rotten apprentice Hero and I drop my sword."

The innkeeper, never letting go of his shoulder, looked the skinny boy over with disfavor. He gave an especial scowl at the cowlick that stood straight up from the unruly brown hair on Halitor's forehead. "If you've no money, you can scrub pots. And comb your hair first." Then he let go Halitor's shoulder, so he could grab the boy's ear.

"Ow!" The innkeeper ignored Halitor's shout and held the ear tighter, marching him down the stairs and through the kitchen. "You're a kitchen boy now, 'til you work off your debt."

Before he knew what was up, Halitor found himself in the kitchen yard with a vast tub of soapy water, a mountain of dirty cookware, and a sore ear. He rubbed his ear and stared at the pots, with no idea how this had happened to him, nor what to do with the dishes.

Halitor's humiliation was complete when the girl who had rescued herself appeared in the yard next to him. Her hair was perfectly combed and tied neatly back from a pale face. She watched him struggle with the dirty pots.

"I didn't know Heroes washed dishes," she said after a time, during which Halitor tried very hard not to notice she was there, and lost his dish-scrubber three times in the murky water.

"They don't," he said without looking up. "I'm not a Hero anymore. I'm just a kitchen boy."

"Oh." She watched while he struggled with a big pot, then reached around him and shoved it into place. She did it with ease, despite being a head shorter than he was.

"Thanks," Halitor said morosely.

She didn't say anything. Nor did she go away, which made him clumsier, as always happened when he got close to anything female. He dropped a kettle on his foot.

Halitor jumped around and swore in three languages and six dialects. Travels with Bovrell had been educational in some ways, if not in the manner intended.

"I didn't know Heroes swore, either," the girl said.

"Kitchen boys curst well do!"

"I'm sorry you aren't a Hero any more. I wanted you to teach me to use a sword."

Halitor dropped the pot again. This time he didn't even bother cursing. "You want me to teach you? But," he swallowed miserably, "I dropped my sword. You're the one who killed that ogre."

"I'm sure it was just beginner's luck. And I'm sure you are a wonderful swordsman when you aren't so nervous, and distracted by your master. Anyway, even a hero-in-training who drops his sword knows more about fighting than a kitchen wench."

Halitor didn't explain that he would always be nervous when rescuing Fair Maidens. Instead, he asked, "You're a kitchen wench?"

"Why else would I be here in the kitchen yard with a mountain of potatoes to peel?"

He hadn't noticed what she was doing, since she made him too nervous to look at her. "You aren't a Princess?"

"Of course not. Princesses don't peel potatoes. I'm a kitchen wench." She picked up a spud and started peeling, as if to prove her point. "Besides, Princesses have long blonde hair." There was no denying hers was a rich dark brown, and not much more than shoulder length.

"But ogres are only supposed to carry off Princesses. *The Hero's Guide to Battles, Rescues, and the Slaying of Monsters* says so."

"Perhaps the ogre was confused. Your master seemed to think like you," she added. "He was all for riding off into the sunset and living happily ever after, until I said I had to get back to scrub the vegetables for dinner or I'd get a licking. Then he couldn't be rid of me fast enough. Said I'd let myself be rescued under false pretenses."

"You rescued yourself. And," he remembered

7

a grievance, "you left me to walk back to town."

She blushed. "I'm sorry about that. It—I—It wasn't a nice thing to do."

"No. It wasn't." Halitor turned back to the mountain of dirty pots. "So, if you please, just leave me alone."

After she left with her basket of peeled potatoes, he thought that he could at least have asked her name.

So Halitor the Hero became Halitor the Kitchen Boy, and his sword rusted in the corner of the stable loft where he slept, while he tried to forget he'd ever dreamed of battles and adventures.

When he wasn't washing pots and hauling water from the well or garbage to the river, or trying to dry his clothes, which were always wet from his slops and spills, he spent his time dodging the girl.

Young men who try to avoid young women are doomed to failure.

The girl, whose name he eventually learned was Melly, always seemed to be somewhere about. When Halitor lagged behind in his pot scrubbing, which he often did because he was not at all good at it, Melly found his missing soap, made him a new scrubbing pad, or took a few pots aside and scrubbed them herself. Since her presence made Halitor so nervous that he dropped even more pans, she worked silently and behind his back, so that after a while he forgot to notice her.

After many, many days of her help, Halitor managed to mutter, "Thanks, Melly." Then he turned bright red and dropped a pot on his foot.

The next day he said it again and turned a little pink, and didn't drop anything at all.

By the end of the week, he could say "Thank you" and not even blush. It helped that Melly always wore ragged and shapeless clothes, so she hardly looked like his idea of a Girl. Not that he looked at her closely enough to tell, not if he could help it. In just a few short weeks of being yelled at by cooks and customers and Derker the Innkeeper, Halitor had learned to keep his head down and not look anyone in the face.

When he got used to her being about, Halitor began to talk to Melly. He had to talk to someone or burst, though he still didn't look at her if he could help it. Because it was most on his mind, he told her how he had ended up a kitchen boy in a scrubby town far from his own scrubby village.

He told her about his father, the village smith. "When I was little, we thought I'd be his apprentice and become the smith after him. Then when I was nine, I set the forge on fire. Ma put it out with her tub of wash water, but Da said I couldn't work there any more. I dropped too many things. And Ma said I couldn't have anything more to do with fire. Her favorite skirt was in that washtub, and it was completely ruined."

"But you never went and did it on purpose!" Melly protested.

"Nay. I tripped. Accidents always happen where I am."

Neither had any answer to that. Halitor had just dropped yet another kettle on his foot, so Melly took and washed it while he hopped about and cursed in the secret language of Kargor, the next country east of his home in Duria.

Over the following weeks he told her his whole story. How from age nine to fourteen he had been offered to every tradesman in the village, and sent back from each within a week because he had broken or spilled or ruined something expensive, or hurt himself. Even the farmers wouldn't have him after he'd stuck a sickle in his own leg. When that was healed, he just moped about the house waiting for something to happen.

"When I was fourteen, Bovrell the Bold saved our village from a giant, chased the monster right off back to the hills. Da somehow convinced him he needed an apprentice, and told me not to move or do anything until I was signed on and away. He said if I came back from this one he'd feed me to the pigs. He told Bovrell I was big and strong and couldn't seem to settle. Since that's most of what you need to be a Hero, and since Da paid him, he took me on. Only," he said with more weariness than bitterness, "to be a Hero you need to be able to use a weapon without hitting your own horse. Or dropping it, or bashing yourself on the helmet and knocking yourself out."

When looked at in that light, Halitor had done rather well in the incident involving Melly and the ogre. But she didn't say anything. She just looked sympathetic, and he kept talking, without noticing how little she said about herself.

After two more weeks, Melly asked, "Halitor, even though you aren't maybe as good as you wish you were, don't you think you could teach me a little about swords and knives and fighting?"

"Do you want to be a Hero?" he said, and laughed. "You know girls can't be Heroes. They have to be Fair Maidens. It would…confuse… things if girls were Heroes and rescued Fair Maidens." His head spun a bit at all the implications.

"I don't want to be a Hero. And I'm not a Fair Maiden, just a kitchen wench. I want to be able to defend myself when there are monsters about." She reminded him of how they met. "I want to be safe even when a Hero decides he doesn't want to waste his time on a kitchen wench."

Halitor was confused, but he couldn't seem to refuse Melly when she asked a favor. She had some mysterious power over him, and thinking about it made him nervous, so he just did as she asked.

That evening when all the pots were washed and the potatoes for breakfast peeled and cut and set to soak in cold water, and the floors scrubbed and the fires laid for morning, Halitor went with Melly to the stable and took his sword from its corner and showed her how to hold it. Because he was thinking about making sure she didn't drop it, he didn't even notice that he held it comfortably.

"It's heavy," he warned her as he handed it over. Melly took it and held it more easily than he had when he began learning. Melly's work in the kitchen—which like Halitor's involved hauling heavy loads about—made her a great deal stronger than she looked, and she had more grace than he expected. She explained that a kitchen wench wasn't at all the same thing as a Fair Maiden, let alone a Princess. A kitchen wench worked for her living and built some muscle doing it. Halitor taught her the simplest sword drill he knew, and fell asleep while she practiced.

After that, they went to the stable every night after work and practiced. It was the end of summer, and there was just enough light in the stable yard still to see what they were doing. As the fall moved on and it grew darker in the evenings, Melly lit a torch and they practiced by its light. Halitor found a barrel-stave and used his belt knife to carve a passable wooden practice sword so that they could spar, once she learned a few basic moves and the cuts he'd gotten on his hands carving it had healed. After she left each night, he practiced more, because soon she was nearly as good as he was. For the first time, having explained it all to someone else, he understood what he needed to do to improve. He only hit himself in the foot once, and since he was using the wooden sword, it only bruised his toes rather than slicing them open.

Halitor wanted to teach her other weapons, too, since she couldn't carry a sword everywhere, even if they could find one for her. Melly turned out to be far better with a knife than he was. Perhaps until now she had battled only vegetables and the fowl for the stewpot, but she knew how to slice, dice, and eviscerate with the best of them. It didn't take a lot for her to learn

12

to use the knife for fighting as well as cooking. Halitor gave up on knives and concentrated on the sword.

All of this worked because Halitor had almost stopped thinking of Melly as a girl. Somewhere during the lessons, he started to think of her just as Melly, or as a sort of little brother. Not that he'd had any brothers or sisters. Halitor's parents had had no more children after they realized what a disaster he was turning out to be. Melly quickly learned what happened whenever Halitor thought about her being a girl, and took care not to remind him. It was common in Loria for a girl who worked in a kitchen to wear breeches. She began to dress like a boy, and took care that neither breeches nor shirts fit too well.

The disguise fit more than one purpose for Melly. She explained to Halitor that it was much easier to wear breeches than to dispose of those who thought that a kitchen wench was something else. Halitor didn't understand what she meant, and kept on scrubbing pots.

CHAPTER TWO: HALITOR THE HOMELESS

When Melly had gained some skill with the sword, she suggested that they needn't stay on at the Drunken Bard.

"The Innkeeper treats us well enough, I suppose," she told Halitor while he scrubbed pots and she peeled her endless pile of potatoes. "But we could do better."

"It would be dishonorable to run away. I have a debt to pay." Even as a Kitchen Boy, Halitor clung to his Hero's rules.

"You worked off your debt long ago. Derker is taking advantage of you."

"Well, what about you? Are you free to leave when you want?"

Melly turned grim. "I was taken by raiders and sold to Derker as a slave. He would say I am his property and cannot leave. I don't agree. We don't believe in slavery where I come from. No one has the right to take another's freedom, and if they take mine, I have the right to take it back. That's what I want you to help me do: take my freedom back."

Halitor opened his mouth, then shut it again. When she put it that way, he couldn't think of a single response. He didn't think the *Hero's Guide* addressed the issue, though he would read it again to be sure. It sounded a lot like a Rescue, and Rescues were his job. Or would have been, he reminded himself, if he was a Hero instead of a kitchen boy.

To put her off, he said, "Let's practice with the swords. Your left swing is still weak."

As the days grew shorter, Melly continued to suggest that they should leave and go find a better place to make a life.

"We should just go, before winter. You can do better than this, Halitor."

"I think I'd do well to stay with anything that makes me a living. It's not like I've been any good at anything else I've ever tried."

"You aren't earning much of a living here, Halitor. And it's not like you're good at scrubbing pots."

Halitor thought that was a bit unkind of her, but he didn't realize that thanks to the daily practice Melly demanded, he had become better with his sword than he was with the pot scrubber. He was too concerned about the fact that Melly was getting better with the sword than he was to see his own improvement. And she already knew more about knives than Halitor did. Bovrell had said knives were an assassin's weapon, not a Hero's, and wouldn't teach him to use them for anything but cutting up their dinner. When Halitor watched Melly use hers, he thought maybe Bovrell hadn't known what he was talking about. Halitor also thought that he was no kind of Hero, if a kitchen wench could use weapons better than he could. He didn't bother saying this. Instead, he distracted her.

15

"I cut us some poles. Let's practice with staffs."

"Good idea," Melly agreed. "You can always find a stick, and a girl never knows when she'll need to keep the scum off."

Halitor didn't know what to say to that, but it was fun working with the staff. And he was beginning to see that Bovrell hadn't been a good teacher.

"That man was too lazy to teach you much of anything," Melly said when Halitor commented on it. She was right. To teach an apprentice like Halitor, as clumsy as he was earnest, had been far too much effort for a man like Bovrell. Earnest boys who were clumsy by nature got clumsier still when they tried too hard. All his life, Halitor had tried very hard at everything.

Now, because Halitor was thinking more about what Melly was doing than about himself, he was much less earnest than usual, and much more successful. Since he had gotten used to her, even if she was a girl, he no longer dropped pots and pans whenever she came around. So, without his noticing, Halitor had become, not a great swordsman (which would be too much to ask), but one who no longer dropped his sword, and who generally hit what he swung at. He began to enjoy sword practice.

Halitor was still sure running off was a bad idea, at least for him.

"I'm no good at things like that," he argued when Melly raised the subject a few days later. "I've failed at Heroing in six different countries. But I've been working here for weeks and they haven't thrown me. Maybe I've found what the gods intended me to be."

"The gods want you to be a kitchen boy?" Melly's scorn hurt, a little. "You really believe that?"

"Well, someone has to scrub pots. It's honest work, anyway." He kicked at the straw that covered the floor of the loft. "I've failed at smithing, tanning, potting, carpentry, farming and heroing. There aren't a lot of professions left."

Melly refused to agree. "You haven't really had a chance. No one would let you try anything long enough to get over being nervous and start to learn. Look how much better you are with the sword, just because you keep practicing." Then she added, "And the only reason they keep you here is that they don't have to pay you."

"I get food and a place to sleep," he protested, turning red. "And I have to pay off Bovrell's debt. He ran up a big bill for ale and spirits."

"I don't see why you should have to pay his bills. Your own, well, I guess you owe that, though as your apprentice-master Bovrell should have paid for you. But why should you pay for his drinks ?"

Halitor opened his mouth to answer, and stopped. Why should he pay Bovrell's bills? "Because I'm his apprentice?" he suggested, trying to convince himself.

"Not any more. Not once he left you. No," she said, "you have long since paid off your own debt, and you should go somewhere you can negotiate a decent wage. Or at least," she looked around the loft, "a real room to sleep in. Back home in Ga-Gandaria," she stuttered over the place name, "workers all get a good place to sleep."

"This isn't so bad," Halitor defended his loft. "It's dry, and the animals down below keep it warm. It's October. It will be cold out there, wherever we go." Where on earth was Gandaria? He thought he'd been just about everywhere with Bovrell, but he'd never even heard of the place.

"It might be warm in here, but it stinks of dung!"

He sniffed. If he thought about it, he supposed it did smell a bit like dung up here. He didn't notice unless he paid attention.

"I guess I've gotten used to it," he said. That seemed to make Melly even madder.

"You've gotten used to living atop a dung-heap? Is that any kind of life?"

"I don't know." He never seemed to have a good answer when she started rearranging his life.

He knew then that in the end he'd go with her. He was getting used to doing what she wanted.

Melly made all the plans. Though she had convinced Halitor they had every right to go, both knew the owner of the Drunken Bard wouldn't agree. Derker still said that Halitor owed money, because his room and board cost nearly as much as his work was worth.

Melly disagreed. And, Halitor was learning, when her mind was made up, a fellow might as well give up arguing.

Melly's position was trickier. She was a slave,

and as a slave, had no right to leave or do much of anything else. Including, Halitor now realized, learn to use weapons. He turned a bit pale when he thought of it.

"I could be in big trouble just for teaching you to fight, couldn't I?"

"Sure, because slaves aren't supposed to use weapons. But no one asked me if I wanted to be a slave, did they?" she asked. "They just snatched me up and hauled me so far from home I couldn't get back and would have to stay where they put me. And then they sold me. They took what was mine and mine only, my freedom and my body and my time, and they sold it and they kept the money. I don't owe any of these people anything."

When Halitor nodded his agreement at last, she added, "But somewhere out there is a bunch of scum I owe a thrashing."

By the time Halitor worked out what she meant, Melly was long gone to her own room, and he went to bed and forgot to worry about it.

A few days later, Melly told Halitor her story.

"Da is a merchant," she said. "At least, I hope he still is." Halitor took a moment to figure out she meant she hoped her Da was still alive, and feared he wasn't. "He's a dealer in wines and cheeses. We traveled from town to town, and he sold his wares. It was just the two of us."

"Didn't you have a mother, or any brothers?"

"No. Just us two." She didn't elaborate, and Halitor felt delicate about asking what had happened to her mother.

"We lived in Gandaria," she said, and this

19

time she didn't stutter over the name, "way up in the north of Garan, and as long as we stayed there we were fine. But one year Da just had to see what the markets were like in the next valley, over in Duria."

"I'm from Duria," Halitor interrupted. Somehow it made him feel closer to Melly, knowing she'd been near his home. Maybe she'd even visited his village.

Melly nodded, but didn't pursue the subject. "We'd had a good trip and were heading back home," she went on, "and that's when the bandits came." She looked away as though it was hard to speak of it. "I think they killed Da," she whispered. "They knocked me out and tied me up and I didn't know anything until I was a long way away. When I came to, I threw up on the leader's boots, and I think that made him decide to get rid of me."

"That might have been a good thing," Halitor said.

She nodded. "Yes. I think that Derker here at the Drunken Bard is greedy and selfish, but he's still human. Zarad, the bandits' leader, stopped being human a long time ago. So they brought me here, and sold me to Derker. I've been here nearly a year, and I've never been able to get word of Da. I thought he'd have come for me by now, if he were alive. So," she dragged a sleeve across her face to wipe away her tears, "I don't suppose I have a home to go to, but I still want to go back."

Feeling bad, even though he had no home where he'd be welcome, and no desire to go back at all, Halitor patted her on the shoulder.

"There, there," he said as though she were a child. "We'll get you home." So, without even realizing it, he committed himself to her escape, and thus to his own.

Melly now had a plan, though she wouldn't tell Halitor what it was. She just said that they must start saving up bread and cheese and bits of gear they'd need on a long walk. They would have no horse. Bovrell had taken Halitor's horse when he left, since it was his horse in any case.

"We could take one," Melly suggested.

"I won't be a horse-thief," Halitor insisted. "Besides, I'd mess it up, and you only get one chance at stealing horses." Justice for horse thieves was swift and permanent. "So we'll have to walk. Anyway, I won't steal," he repeated.

"I wouldn't stop at stealing a horse from these unspeakably greedy and heartless people—" Melly had taken to speaking thus of the inn-keeper and his wife—"but they would chase us harder if we stole a horse, and it's harder to hide, and much worse if we're caught. So I suppose our feet will have to do."

When they had a good store of food saved up, Melly told Halitor the plan, or at least as much as he needed to know to get started. By now he was so used to following her "suggestions" that he didn't even think of questioning her. She told him to be ready at midnight, so at midnight he waited in his loft with two rough packs, one much larger than the other. When she came, she looked at the small pack he handed her.

"What's this?"

"I would have carried everything, but I

thought it might be better if you had some food and a blanket. Just in case." He didn't say in case of what.

She looked at him and put on the pack. That's when he realized that not only was she wearing her boys' clothes—a rough shirt and breeches just like his own—but she'd cut her hair short. She saw him looking.

"It's better if I'm a boy. Otherwise—well, you know." He wasn't sure he did, but figured she knew best. "Besides, only boys carry these." She turned so that he could see the sword hanging at her belt. It was real, and looked like a good one. He checked to be sure she hadn't stolen his and left him with the wooden practice sword, but she had gotten hers somewhere else.

Halitor opened his mouth, but closed it again without asking his question. Some things he really didn't want to know. If someone was going to come looking for the sword, though, he wanted to be far away.

"Follow me," Melly said unnecessarily.

They walked all through the remainder of that night and on into the next day, until they stopped to eat lunch. After they ate, Halitor insisted on a rest, lest they drop in their tracks. Melly would have gone on, but the sun on her back took effect before she could get up, and she fell asleep in the middle of telling Halitor not to be a big baby.

He sat and kept watch for a while, before he, too, fell asleep.

When they woke up, the warm and pleasant midday had turned into a chilly and damp late afternoon. Halitor sat up with a groan.

"Ugh. I'm cold and stiff, and we've wasted most of the afternoon," he grumbled. "Why couldn't you stay awake?"

"Why couldn't you stay awake?" Melly climbed to her feet as though her whole body had gone stiff and sore, just like Halitor. "You were the one who said we had to rest," she added.

"I didn't mean we should sleep all afternoon!"

"Oh, forget it. Let's start walking. No one found us, and walking will warm us up, so I guess maybe it didn't matter." Melly managed to say it like another complaint, rather than a consolation. Mumbling under his breath about kitchen wenches who thought they knew everything, Halitor followed her up the trail. They kept walking until they were warm, by which time they were far from Carthor and the Drunken Bard, and nearing the border with Arania. Far off in the distance they could see the foothills of the Ice Castle, many days walk to the north.

When night fell they were still walking, and Halitor knew they'd chosen the wrong time to run away. Not the wrong time of day, but the wrong time of year. It wasn't winter, but in these lands, frost came early. It was cold. Halitor looked up at the gathering clouds with suspicion. It looked to him like rain.

Melly halted at last, wrapping her arms around herself and shivering. "We need a place to spend the night."

Halitor didn't answer, but looked around

until he spotted an overgrown path leading away from the stream. As he hoped, it ended at an empty barn. There was a farmhouse, but it was empty too. Everything was overgrown, with a sad, abandoned air. They continued to shiver while they ate a bit more of their bread and cheese. Then Halitor gathered what hay was left in the barn into two very separate piles, and they wrapped themselves in their blankets and went to sleep at once, worn out from walking half the night and most of the day.

Long before morning the cold awakened them both, to toss and turn and doze until the sun came up. Then they rose too, to argue over whose fault it was they were so cold, until the heat of the argument made them warm, which proved that even bad behavior can have its uses.

"I knew running off was a bad idea," Halitor said. "'Let's run off so we won't be worked to death,' you said. We won't be worked to death, because we'll be dead of the cold instead!"

"If you weren't a chivalrous fool we could keep each other warm just fine!"

They left the barn still arguing. Halitor was so befuddled by this that he didn't notice that while they argued, Melly was leading them farther along their way. Away from the town and the inn, away from food and warmth and dirty dishes and orders.

On the third day away from the Drunken Bard, they remembered that the foothills were the realm of ogres, giants, and dragons. They remembered because the ogres found them.

CHAPTER 3: ENCOUNTERS WITH OGRES

Melly clutched Halitor's arm and pointed into the woods. A pair of small ogres stared at them, growling and gnashing their teeth. When the young people drew their swords, the ogres slunk away. Ogres wouldn't attack people who could put up a fight. Still, after that, Melly and Halitor walked a little faster and a little closer together. The next ogres might not be so quick to take flight. It began to drizzle, and Halitor thought of his stable loft. If not for Melly, he would have been there, warm and dry, and with a full belly.

"We need to get onto a main road," Melly said. "There's bound to be more monsters about and I don't want to meet them."

"What about Derker? Won't he be looking on the road for us?"

"Not in the rain, not him. And anyway, he'll think we've gone south, or off by the Great Road. Not up towards the Ice Castle with winter coming on."

Halitor didn't much like the sound of that, but he liked the idea of following a road, where more traffic might mean fewer ogres. They found a path that after much winding joined the road, and turned again toward the mountains.

Around noon they smelled the smoke of a cooking fire—smoke mingled with something that made Halitor's stomach growl.

"I bet it's a trader's caravan," Melly whispered, peeking around a tree at the camp where half a dozen wagons were stopped for a mid-day meal. "Maybe we can join them, if they're going our way."

Halitor remembered that she and her Da had been traders. She must be used to that sort of thing. "I'll go in first," he said, trying to think what a Hero would do. "What if they're slave-hunters, or bandits?" Melly nodded, as though Halitor could somehow protect her. He knew that if they were bandits, the most he could do was occupy them long enough for her to escape. Well, that was something, and it was what a Hero would do.

The merchants were just merchants, and shared their meal in exchange for news. They would have preferred coin, but there was much the young travelers did not have, and coins were among them. The caravan-master was a kindly sort, so he let them eat. They looked like a pair of boys out for adventure and discovering it to be hungry work, as well as cold and wet. He asked about the road ahead, on down across Loria to Carthor and the other towns.

Halitor and Melly, disappointed the caravan wasn't going their way, told what they could about the road, without mentioning that they hadn't been using it.

When they parted, the caravan master warned them, "Ye'd do well to take care. Find a caravan if ye can. The ogres are bad this year."

"Were you attacked?" Halitor asked, feeling to be sure his sword was still in place.

"Nay, not us. They won't attack a large party, seein' as they can't work together, not more than two at a time anyhow. A pair of younglings like ye, though, they might think were easy pickins."

Melly thanked him for his concern, and, hitching her sword to a more comfortable position under her hand, promised they'd be careful. "We can't wait for another group. We are in a bit of a hurry."

"Ay. Ye'd best move on fast in any case. It's fair cold up high, and the weather has a changing feel. This rain could turn to snow up there any time, if it hasn't already."

Halitor felt a deeper chill than the drizzle caused. Until now he hadn't grasped that their way led through a high pass. Melly led him off before he could ask any more questions.

They kept a sharp, nervous eye out front and back after they started on. After a mile or so, however, they started arguing again and forgot to watch.

"Why do we have to cross the mountains, anyway?" Halitor asked.

"Because my home lies on the other side," Melly answered, in that too-patient voice that means both parties are about to be aggravated.

"But why can't we go south? We could take the Great Road," he suggested, referring to the largest road that linked the valley states of Loria, Garan, Duria and Kargor, which spread out from the Ice Castle like the splayed fingers of a hand. "Or even the desert route." He and Bovrell had gone around the south end of the range that separated Duria and Garan, and it had been warm, even in the dead of winter. Maybe her home—what had she called it? Gandaria?—was in the far north. That would explain why he'd never heard of it.

"How long did all that riding around take you?" Melly asked in a tone that didn't encourage him to answer. He did anyway.

"I don't know, maybe a few months? We did stuff along the way, you know."

He wanted to tell her that they had rescued maidens and freed a village from a cruel overlord. And they had done those things, but Halitor had always dropped his sword or ridden the wrong way or fallen from his horse. Every single time. By the time they had reached Loria and rescued Melly, Bovrell was scarcely speaking to him. He didn't want to talk about it.

"Say, Melly," he said to change the subject, since the idea of going south didn't seem to go over well, especially as they had walked north for three days already and would have to go back towards Carthor and the Inn. "I never did ask how you got taken by that ogre in the first place. I mean, if you were at the inn and all." Ogres would never come into a town, though according to the *Hero's Guide* they might enter a lone castle to take a princess.

"I, um," she glanced at him and went ahead and said it. "I was trying to run off."

The news didn't shock or surprise him as it might have once. After all, they were running away now because she wanted to. Of course she'd tried before. He thought of something else. "Ogres are only supposed to kidnap Princesses.

The Guide says so. So why you?"

"Maybe they only kidnap princesses, but I'm pretty sure they'll eat anyone." She sighed. "I suppose that was what it would have done. How should I know?"

Halitor didn't answer, because he didn't know how to tell if an ogre was kidnapping a Princess or looking for dinner. And what did they do with the ones who weren't rescued? It wasn't like the ogres did it just so Heroes could have someone to rescue. That wouldn't be a good bargain for the ogres, who nearly always ended up killed by the Heroes, if the Guide was right.

Thinking made his head hurt, so he stopped thinking and went back to watching for ogres. Fighting monsters he understood, even if he wasn't any good at it.

Perhaps because the caravan had just passed through and scared them all off, Halitor and Melly saw no more ogres that day. When the sun went down, they realized they had a new problem. By now they were well up in the mountains, beyond the farmed lands, and that meant no abandoned farms, and no barn to huddle in for the night. The rain had stopped, but everything was wet, including them, and it was cold.

"Maybe we can find a cave?" Melly suggested with less confidence than she'd ever shown to Halitor.

"Do ogres live in caves?" Halitor asked. Neither knew the answer to that, so they stood on the road and looked around blankly.

"In any case," Melly said after a bit, "I don't see any caves around here." That was true. All

29

around them grew a thick forest, still dripping from the rain that had fallen all day. It was already deep dusk under the trees.

"We could just walk all night," Halitor suggested, a little afraid of what she might say. Melly nodded. "Would it be too hard?" he asked.

"We did it the first night," she said.

Halitor thought that after a night and a day on the road she looked more tired than she had then, but he decided perhaps he would not say so. Instead, he said, "We can wrap our blankets around us like cloaks and we'll keep warm enough, walking."

She nodded and hitched her pack to a new position. Halitor wanted to offer to carry her pack, which he thought must hurt her shoulders, but he didn't do that, either. Melly, he felt certain, would tell him to stop treating her like a helpless Princess.

It was funny how scornful she was of Princesses. Sometimes Halitor thought she must wish she were one.

After an hour or so the moon, which had been full the night they ran away, came up. When it shone between the clouds, it added enough light to see the road, and they could walk faster, but in some ways it made visibility worse. The silvery light cast deep and eerie shadows. Before, there hadn't been shadows, just darkness. Now, the moonlight filtered through the trees here and there, illuminating this bush or that stump. Every third tree looked like an ogre. And when the clouds covered the moon, it was so dark they couldn't see at all.

When they met a real ogre, they had grown so used to seeing a monster in every bush that they dismissed the bulging shadow as just another illusion. They'd long since stopped asking each other, "does that look like an ogre to you?" because however much it looked like an ogre, it never turned out to be one.

They were wiser now and knew it was just a shadow or a stump, right up to the moment when the shadow reached out to grab at Melly. She smelled its fetid ogre-breath just in time, and dodged away with a scream that warned Halitor.

He turned around, and didn't see the ogre who, puzzled by the fact that the boy he'd grabbed screamed like a girl, had stopped moving to figure it out, turning himself back into a stump. Halitor kept turning, tangling himself in his blanket, and struggled to draw his sword.

Melly didn't wait. But though Halitor knew the wise thing was to run, she already had her sword out and was on the attack. He forgot that a Hero is always polite.

"Run, Melly, you fool!"

She planted her feet in the ready stance he had taught her, and made no move to run. Halitor sighed, but by now it was too late. If the ogre had been confused by Melly's boyish clothing and girlish scream, it recovered quickly. Halitor knew from the Guide that to an ogre, people were dinner. Nor was this ogre intimidated by their swords, unlike the ones they'd met that morning. It was a great deal larger, too.

The ogre lumbered toward the girl.

Melly stood firm, her sword at the ready.

31

Halitor struggled to untangle himself and his sword from his blanket-cloak, and readied himself to die in defense of a Fair Maiden, even if she wasn't a Princess.

By the time he could move to plant himself alongside Melly, she was swinging and stabbing at the ogre, which dodged her blows or deflected them with armored armbands, and kept right on coming. It would have her in a moment.

"Oh, no, you don't!" Halitor yelled, and lunged at the creature. His foot caught in the blanket he had just dropped, and he fell, arms flailing in an effort to keep his balance. The thrust he'd meant as a killing blow to the monster's heart first slashed off a few fingers, then came down with all Halitor's weight behind it, pinning an unprotected and surprisingly sensitive ogre foot to the ground. The ogre let out a howl that echoed off the sides of the valley.

Halitor, dazed by his fall, lay on the ground gasping as the creature turned its attention to him, forgetting about Melly.

That was all the opening she needed. Melly grasped her sword with both hands and swung. She struck where the armored body met the stone-hard head, and sliced right through the narrow band of vulnerable flesh, spraying herself and Halitor with green blood. The headless ogre toppled as Halitor struggled to his feet.

"Oy," he croaked. "Aiee."

Melly stood looking from the headless corpse to the round head still rolling down the road, and gulped twice. Then she swayed and collapsed. Halitor caught her just before she hit the ground.

"I don't think we did so well," Halitor said gloomily. He was nursing a sputtering fire while Melly shivered under both their blankets. Halitor had carried her and all their gear a quarter mile up the road and found a small clearing just off the trail. Someone had camped there before, and left a ring of burnt stones. Then Halitor had spent a long time finding a bit of dryish wood under the thick-branched fir trees, and even longer coaxing it to burn. He didn't think they were going any farther until morning, and they needed warmth.

Melly pulled the blankets more tightly around her. She'd been shivering ever since she came out of her swoon.

"The ogre is dead and we are alive," she pointed out, in response to Halitor's assessment.

"I tripped on my own blanket and fell on my face." His cheeks were hotter than the fire justified.

"And I swooned," Melly agreed. "But you did stab him, and distracted him so I could behead him."

He felt a little better. She made it sound almost like they'd planned it. And he hadn't dropped his sword.

"And you didn't pass out until it was over," he said, to make sure she didn't feel bad either.

"Right."

"You didn't pass out at all the other time," he said.

"No. It wasn't so messy that time. Cutting off the head was," she swallowed hard, "it wasn't what I expected."

33

He nodded. He'd not expected so much blood either. Some of it was still on them. He could feel it and wished they could wash it off. Maybe in the morning.

The fire was burning better now. He added a larger stick. "Can I have a blanket?"

"No."

Halitor looked at her, surprised. It wasn't like Melly to be greedy.

She held one side of the blanket out to him. "We'll be warmer if we share." When he hesitated, she added, "Come on. I won't attack you, and I don't have cooties. I just want to be warm."

Halitor was pretty sure the heat burning in his face would keep them both warm, but he threw another stick on the fire anyway, before he sat down next to her and wrapped the blanket around them both. It was warmer that way. Once again, he vowed to stay awake and keep watch.

CHAPTER 4: HERE BE DRAGONS

The sun rose late through the icy morning mists, until it got bright enough to wake Halitor and Melly. Halitor was cold and stiff, and hauling Melly up the road and into the forest to find a camp had strained muscles he couldn't name. She might be skinny, but she was no featherweight. He didn't know if it was because of the muscles Melly had developed as a kitchen-wench, or if all girls were heavier than they looked. Bovrell had always carried away the Fair Maidens they rescued, lest Halitor drop them.

Melly sat up with a groan a moment later. Their fire was out and there was frost on the ground, and she was shivering again. At least it wasn't raining, or snowing.

"What is there for breakfast?" Her teeth chattered as she spoke.

Halitor looked in his pack, then hers. He took everything out of each and looked again. "We have three bits of stale bread, but all the cheese is gone. We're going to be more hungry before we're less, I think." He went to build a new fire. Melly got up and took their one little pot, which she'd "borrowed" from the kitchen at The Drunken Bard, and went to find a stream.

They used the hot water to wash down the stale bread. It made the bread easier to swallow and warmed them some, even if it did nothing to ease their hunger. Halitor thought about life at the Drunken Bard. They hadn't paid him, but they had fed him every day. He missed that. He missed being warm, too. He'd never been this miserable when he rode with Bovrell. Bovrell the Bold didn't visit places without inns.

They didn't linger over breakfast, since there was so little to eat. Halitor swallowed the last of his warm water and moved closer to the fire.

"We should get started. I don't know how far it is to the pass, but I want to be over and well down the other side before nightfall."

Melly nodded, and also moved closer to the fire. "Maybe tonight we could find—well, not an inn, because an inn would want money, but maybe a stable or a barn or even an old hay-stack. Even a haystack would be warmer than this place." She quickly added, "Though you did well to find anyplace at all to camp, in the dark and all."

"I think it's going to be sunny," Halitor noted, turning to warm his back at the fire.

"The weather could change any minute up here," she reminded him as she went to refill the pot. Halitor rolled the blankets, and watched as Melly poured the potful of water on the fire. With no more fire, there was no reason to stay.

They walked with their hands on their sword hilts, watching for ogres. For a while, Halitor tried holding his sword at the ready, but his arm soon grew so tired he thought he wouldn't be able to swing it if they were attacked. Twice he almost dropped it when he stumbled on a root or a rock. So he put the sword back in the scabbard, and hoped he'd be able to draw it in time if they were attacked. It was still chilly, but neither suggested wearing their blankets. They just set a brisk pace and waited for the exercise and sun to warm them.

The road, which had climbed gradually the previous day, now rose sharply, as though in a hurry to deliver them to the heights. It got steeper and steeper, and walking was hard work. Once the sun was well up, Halitor stopped shivering and started sweating. Melly soon turned a rosy pink, and Halitor saw her wipe her forehead with a sleeve. If she were a Princess, she wouldn't be sweating. The *Hero's Guide* was clear on that. In Chapter Six, "All About Princesses," it said, "A princess will never perspire, as that would be indelicate." As sweat dripped from his nose and stung his eyes, Halitor wondered how princesses kept cool. Maybe they just never worked hard enough to warm up. Maybe there wasn't anything special about being a princess at all. That was a curious thought. But questioning the Guide seemed wrong, so he tried to think about something else.

They didn't see any ogres. At first he thought maybe they had frightened them off, with their quick and decisive victory the night before. By the time they stopped for lunch, Halitor was pretty sure they were too high up for ogres. The monsters couldn't build fires, and they didn't wear much clothing, though they did wear armor—unless that was part of their skin. The Guide didn't say, as far as he could recall. Without fires or clothes, ogres would freeze so high in the mountains. And what—or who—would they eat?

The pines here were shorter and more gnarled, and grew farther apart. Melly said that was what happened when you went high in the mountains. In the far north, on the Ice Castle's higher slopes, there were no trees at all. Just ice.

"It's a lot higher than this little pass."

"Have you seen the Ice Castle?" Halitor asked. "Is it really a great castle of ice?"

"No, silly," Melly said. "It's a mountain. A mountain covered with snow and ice. I suppose someone just thought it looked like a big shiny white castle. But no," she added, "I've not seen it. I just—I listen a lot when people talk."

As the road climbed it narrowed, until it was just wide enough for a merchant's cart. They met no other travelers, and the path was not well worn. Sometimes they caught glimpses of the pass ahead. Halitor thought it looked high enough. He didn't need to go so high nothing would grow and everything would be covered with ice. That morning had been icy enough for him. Maybe he wouldn't become a Yeti-herder after all.

When they stopped for lunch—the last bits of stale bread—they found a rock outcrop with a wide view of the valley they were leaving. Far down the valley they could just make out the towers of Carthor, where the Drunken Bard stood. It didn't look like such a great town from this distance.

"Gads," Halitor said, looking over it all, his jaw hanging a bit loose.

Melly glanced at him. "You'd think you never looked down on a valley before. And you with all your travels!" She removed her sword and pack so she could rest more comfortably.

He shook his head. "I haven't, not like this. I think Bovrell is afraid of heights, or of mountains, or something. We always either crossed the mountains on the Great Road, or went around through the desert. I don't think we ever went anywhere as high and wild as this."

"But the monsters live in the mountains," Melly protested. "How could you go around rescuing Fair Maidens if you never went near the mountains?"

"Oh, well." Halitor didn't look at her. "Sometimes we went a little into them. Mostly we rescued Fair Maidens in the valleys. Or the foothills."

"Well, I never!" Melly said it exactly like the cook at the Drunken Bard. Even a kitchen wench could be rendered speechless, if only for a moment. "So all that travel and you've hardly been off the Great Road?"

He shook his head.

"Does this bother you?" she asked a moment later, gesturing at the void beneath their feet, which dangled over the edge of the rock. It was a long way down.

"Should it?" Halitor asked, looking down. "No. I think I like it. It's not so crowded-feeling as the forest. No one can sneak up on us here."

If Halitor had been a more experienced Hero, or if he had had a better teacher, he would have known better than to say that. Any Hero with any real understanding of the job knew that saying "all safe here" or anything like that was the signal for every ogre, dragon, giant or natural disaster in the neighborhood to descend on you.

So when Halitor compounded his error by falling asleep in the warm sun atop the rock, the inevitable happened. Melly was already dozing when he lay down, and neither felt the shadow that passed over them, or heard the whoosh of immense wings. The first Halitor knew of trouble was a yelp from Melly.

Unfortunately, since she had been asleep when the dragon swooped down, her yelp came several seconds after the immense dragon plucked her from the rock, leaving Halitor behind, along with her pack and sword.

He leapt to his feet and brandished his sword, though the dragon was well out of range. When he yelled, "Let her go, you big bully!" Melly screamed, "No, don't! It's a long way down, you fool!"

The dragon ignored them both and swept in a great turn over their rock and headed for the heights, Melly clutched in its great talons.

All Halitor could do was stand on his rock and watch them fly out of sight. Then he picked up the two packs and both swords and scrambled back to the road. There he turned and trudged up toward the pass, where the dragon had vanished with Melly. He had to get her back, but how?

Maybe the dragon laired at the top of the pass. Or nested, or denned, or whatever dragons did. What else did they do? Halitor pulled out the Guide and scanned the section on dragons. They came in all colors, it said, and grew as large as a cottage. They lived on heights and flew down to wreck castles and burn villages, with a fiery breath if you could believe the stories. Halitor had never seen a dragon, and even now hadn't gotten a very good look. It was large, he had seen that much, though it was not as large as a cottage. And it had scales that flashed blue and green in the sun as it flew.

Bovrell had slain one once, in Kargor. He'd made Halitor stay behind in town that day. He said an apprentice would be a liability in a battle with a dragon, especially an apprentice like Halitor. Halitor, looking at the Guide and thinking about what had just happened, wondered if Bovrell really had fought a dragon that day. He'd come back with a Fair Maiden, to be sure, but now that he'd seen a dragon, Halitor thought any Hero who fought one would come out looking a little shopworn, even if he won, especially if dragons did breathe fire. Bovrell's tunic had been as neat and clean on returning as when he'd set out.

Whatever Bovrell had done, Halitor would have to fight this dragon, if he could find it. Tradition said he would walk straight up to the dragon's lair—or nest, or den—just as the dragon was about to do something dreadful to the Fair Maiden—in this case, to Melly. Halitor hoped the dragon knew the rules. What if it got tired of waiting and ate her, or roasted her, or something nasty, before he could climb the hill and find its cave?

Not that it would matter if he did get there in time, he thought as he panted up the road. He couldn't even kill an ogre on his own. The

41

dragon would roast him, and then eat them both. But a Hero had to rescue a Fair Maiden in distress, or die trying. That was the rule. And even though he had nearly given up back at the inn, Halitor still wanted to be a Hero.

At the pass Halitor found a trail of sorts, littered with broken branches and uprooted trees, leading away from the road. Someone had put up a crudely-lettered sign reading "Drawgownes Lare," with an arrow pointing toward a rocky slope. Halitor thought it looked like a trap. Could dragons spell? Why would anyone put up such a sign, except to lure foolish Heroes? What could he do? His actions were all predetermined by *The Hero's Guide to Battles, Rescues, and the Slaying of Monsters*. Thanks to that, he knew just what he must do. Unfortunately, the Guide was thin on information about how to do it. He took off his pack, pulled out the Guide, and thumbed through the dog-eared book to read again what it said about dragons.

Dragons once had the gift of speech with humans, or so it is said. They do not speak now, though they seem to understand much. They are intelligent, at least as much so as dogs. No one is certain why they capture princesses and fair maidens, unless for the accumulation of wealth.

That wasn't much help. He paged through the rest of the section on dragons and found no useful advice. Frustrated, Halitor stowed the book and put both packs back on. Then he left the road and began scrambling over the broken trees that littered the path to the rocky slope he glimpsed ahead. He stopped before the forest ended, and peered out. He was pretty sure, whatever the Guide said, that a smart Hero did some looking about before rushing in. He needed any edge he could get.

Halitor studied the hillside. It was almost a cliff, but a person could climb it. And yes, there was a cave of sorts, with a level place before it. On that level spot sat Melly, and lying with its forelegs around her was the dragon.

The dragon, however, didn't seem to be eating Melly, nor roasting her. Nor was it watching for the inevitable arrival of an avenging Hero. Halitor gazed up at the ledge. The dragon lay with its head drooping and—Halitor crept a little closer to be sure—yes, its eyes nearly closed.

He retreated into the trees and thought about that. Then he snuck around to where the trees grew closest to the cave. He was so absorbed in what he saw that he didn't even notice that for once he didn't step on any branches, and he didn't trip.

He didn't realize, either, that he was not following the usual Hero pattern of rushing right in, a pattern that (though Halitor didn't know it yet) was the main reason there were so few old Heroes, except ones like Bovrell who spent more time drinking in inns than battling monsters.

Halitor stood still among the trees and listened hard. After a few minutes, he realized what he was hearing. He couldn't make out the words, but the tone and rhythm of her speech carried him back to when he was a small boy and his mother would still speak to him.

43

Melly was telling the dragon a bedtime story.

What's more, it was working. The great, ugly head was sinking lower and lower onto the outstretched foreleg, and the huge eyes closed. Halitor stayed where he was and didn't move, for what seemed like hours. He wished he could hear. What sort of bedtime story did a Fair Maiden tell a dragon? And—the thought made him sweat a little—if it fell asleep, shouldn't a Hero rush in and cut off its head?

He concentrated his thoughts on Melly, hoping she would sense he was there and send some sort of signal, but she never looked his way.

Just before sunset, when the dragon's snores began to echo about the pass, Melly slipped slowly and smoothly from its grip. The beast never stirred as she crawled to the brink and peered over. Then she lowered herself off the ledge and onto the rocks. Halitor wanted to run and help her, but was he afraid to move and make a noise which would wake the dragon. So he stayed put and watched.

Melly climbed down the rocks, testing each hold and step before she moved, and Halitor thought it took forever for her to reach the trees. Impatient to be off to someplace safer, he fought the urge to fidget. He was afraid even to let his clothes rustle, despite the dragon's deep snores.

When Melly finally stepped into the forest shadows, he whispered, "Psst! Over here!" She started and made a sound that was almost a squeal, but she managed to stifle it to just a small squeak.

"Sorry," Halitor whispered. "I thought you knew I was here."

"Halitor?! What took you so long?"

"I've been here for ages. I was waiting for you to finish." Before she could find anything to say to that, he added, "Hadn't we better get away from here?" They'd be spending another night high on the pass in any case, but he didn't want to be close by when the dragon woke up. And it was growing cold.

Melly opened her mouth, glanced back at the huge dark shadow of the sleeping dragon, and closed it again. She followed Halitor through the woods and back to the road, both moving as quietly as they could. The sun had set and there was just enough light to keep from crashing into trees or stepping on branches and leaves.

At the road, Halitor paused. He looked at the empty track, looked at Melly, and gave her back her pack and sword.

She put them on. "Why didn't you come to my rescue?" She had to trot to catch up with Halitor as she said it, because he was already striding off down the road as fast as he could walk.

"It looked like you were doing well enough. I was going to go cut its head off once it was asleep, but you climbed down before I could climb up, and it seemed smarter to get away. Can dragons fly at night?"

"How should I know?" Melly said, and added, "It's a fine thing, when a Hero just watches the Fair Maiden rescue herself! Again."

"You're better at it than I am," Halitor admitted. "I'm a lousy Hero. I told you that before we started. If you wanted a real Hero, you should have waited for someone other than a rejected

45

apprentice!"

"I just wish I had!" she snapped.

Halitor picked up the pace until he was almost running. He wished he could get away from this girl, who didn't even want him. But Melly matched his speed and stayed right behind him, though she didn't speak again.

Neither said anything until it was too dark to see the road. By then they were moving more slowly. Halitor tripped three times, but Melly let him catch himself. If she tripped, he didn't know, because he didn't turn around to check on her. Sometime after the last light was gone, Halitor stopped altogether.

"I don't think we can go on. It must be a long way to the nearest farm."

Melly made a sound that might have been a sigh of relief, but Halitor didn't believe that. She probably was just sorry she'd have to spend another night with him. She didn't say one way or the other, nor apologize for being mean. She just ignored the whole quarrel, so he did too.

"A fire would be nice," she said. "It's cold, and I think most monsters are scared of fire."

"Except dragons."

"Then we'd better hope they don't fly at night, because I'm freezing and we need a fire!"

Since it was now too dark to do more than just make out the road, they couldn't find a place to camp. In the end, they stopped by a dead tree and used the dry wood to build a fire right in the middle of the road. As far as they could tell, there'd been no traffic on the road all day, and no one with any sense traveled at night.

Halitor resolved to be up and away as soon as

they could see in the morning. And this time he'd keep watch. A Hero had no business sleeping when he had charge of a Fair Maiden in monster territory. Anyway, he was too hungry to sleep.

CHAPTER 5: HALITOR THE HAPLESS AGAIN

Halitor awoke gradually. The sun wasn't up, but the dawn light was enough to disturb his sleep. He could tell he'd been asleep for several hours, despite his intention to remain awake and feed the fire. It must have gone out long ago. The morning was cold and damp.

He hadn't been awakened by the cold. Halitor discovered he was warm and comfortable wrapped in his thin, damp blanket. He was more warm than comfortable, actually, for the ground was still hard and lumpy, but there was no denying he was warm. Very warm.

Too warm.

Halitor didn't want to open his eyes, not because he wanted to stay asleep and keep dreaming he was warm, but because he didn't want to see what he was pretty sure he was going to see when he did open them.

He opened his eyes. Halitor didn't know it, but it was one of the bravest things he'd done in his life. He opened his eyes and looked right into the huge, multi-colored, oblong eyes of a dragon. Presumably the dragon, the one they'd just escaped. He didn't know how to tell dragons apart, and wasn't interested in learning. He just wanted to know if it was better to pretend he was still asleep and die that way, or to jump up with his sword and die fighting. He knew what the Hero Code said, but he was hungry, miserable, and in the clutches of a dragon. In the face of all that, he had little confidence in the Hero Code or the Guide. Maybe he could die in his sleep if he tried really hard. Halitor supposed a real Hero wouldn't think like that, but he did. He wasn't more than half awake, and lying there waiting to be crisped up like his mother's morning toast did little to clarify his thinking.

After what seemed a long time, Halitor realized that though he was warm, he wasn't being roasted, and opened his eyes again, just a little. The dragon wasn't looking at him now. It was looking at Melly, across the dead fire that they didn't need because the dragon radiated heat like a furnace.

Now was his chance. Just jump up and grab his sword and cut off the dragon's head—or more likely be roasted as he tried to untangle self and sword from the blanket.

Fortunately, before Halitor could do more than push back his blanket a few inches—he didn't need it now anyway, thanks to the dragon—Melly hissed, "Don't move!"

Being used to doing whatever she said, he lay still and watched. Melly sat looking at the dragon, and then she began to talk, in the sort of voice Halitor had heard girls use when talking to puppies or kittens or babies.

"You poor old thing! Did you just want a bit of love, hey? Or another story?" The creature inclined its massive head in a sort of nod, and she reached up to rub the ridge above its eyes. It

49

began making a noise. Halitor would have called it a purr, if something that big and terrifying could purr, which of course it couldn't, being a huge and terrifying fire-breathing monster. But if it could, that dragon was purring.

"How did you know?" he began to ask.

Melly cut him off. "Not now!" Her command was reinforced by a hitch in the purring sound, and a twitch of the big head.

Halitor tried to remember what the Guide said about dragons and their intelligence. There'd been something about them understanding speech. He lay back down and kept as still as possible, while Melly spun a seemingly endless tale of a Princess kidnapped by bandits and forced to suffer all sorts of miseries before being rescued by a beautiful dragon. Halitor thought it was all nonsense—Heroes, not dragons, rescued Princesses!—but he supposed flattery worked well enough on dragons. Just like on boys, a little voice in his head suggested, remembering that he had been contented enough to remain a kitchen boy, until Melly got hold of him and began talking of Heroes and rescues.

After what felt like hours, he heard Melly ask the dragon, "Will you fly us to my home?"

That would shorten the walk, Halitor thought, if they didn't fall off and end up as smears on the rocks or fertilizer in someone's field. And it was nice of her—maybe—to want to include him. Though he thought he might prefer to walk.

While Halitor thought about it, the dragon turned and waddled away a bit before spreading its wings and leaping rather clumsily into the air. The resulting draft blew up a dust storm and scattered the ashes of their fire. When they finished coughing and choking, Melly said, "I think they do better if they can launch themselves off something."

"I guess he didn't want to be our steed." Halitor didn't look at her as he shook the dirt out of his blanket and stowed it in his pack. Breakfast was easy, as they didn't have any. They scattered the remains of their cold fire and started walking. Without the dragon, it was chilly.

After such a long story they weren't making a very early start after all, and they had nothing to eat, but they were alive. Halitor thought that was a fair exchange.

In the afternoon Halitor began to worry they'd have to camp again, and still without anything to eat. His head felt strange. He couldn't think straight, and occasionally a wave of dizziness made him stumble. He didn't mention it to Melly, for fear she'd think him weak, or else joke that he never could think straight, which he had to admit was all too true. They both stumbled more than usual as they pushed on. At last, well into the afternoon, the forest gave way to fields, and they could see a farm house in the distance.

At the sight of the farm, their truce crumbled. Halitor wanted to buy some food from the farmer, but a pale Melly reminded him that they had no money. That left them with a choice between begging and stealing—a choice neither of them liked.

51

"A Hero can't steal. It's goes against everything Heroing is about."

"Well, I'm not going to starve and I'm not going to beg."

"I suppose a kitchen wench is too proud to beg, but you don't mind stealing?"

"I never said I'd steal. And you and your Hero business don't seem to be getting us very far. I suppose you'll go and beg for food?"

"I'm certainly not going to starve! A Hero doesn't beg or steal. A Hero pays his way."

"Oh, yes, with all that coin you're carrying! I'd rather starve than beg, and we assuredly will, if we wait for you to have coin enough for our meals, O Mighty Hero."

"Look who's talking. Proud as a Princess, you are!"

They might have bickered all night, or until they fainted from hunger, if the cottage door hadn't opened. Melly closed her mouth in the middle of a declaration that she'd steal before she'd beg and she'd starve before she'd do either. She stared at the old woman peering around the edge of the door, and turned even paler.

"Fer the love of Gathros, stop that clacking and come eat! If'n yer squeamish about charity, ye'ens can do my chores." The woman's voice started out strong, but developed a quaver so that by the time she finished she sounded even older than she looked.

Halitor looked at Melly to see what she thought, just in time to catch her as she turned a ghastly color and collapsed. The old woman held the door wide, and Halitor figured the argument was over. A Hero couldn't beg, but he could accept charity freely offered. Halitor carried Melly inside and laid her where the woman indicated.

Inside, the house—hut, really, though it looked like luxury after a week of sleeping in the woods—was dim, neat, and smelled of good cooking. Even if the woman was a witch or a bandit or a monster in disguise, Halitor was determined to get some of that food and die happy.

"Sh—he is awful hungry," Halitor said, remembering just a hair too late that Melly was supposed to be a boy. Not that there was any harm in an old woman, but he thought he'd better practice. He mopped Melly's face awkwardly with the cloth the crone handed him, and Melly's eyes opened. She looked past him, closed her eyes again, and took a long, slow breath. Then she opened them and let Halitor help her sit up.

Melly's gaze flew about the room for a moment as though seeking escape, then she smiled at the old woman.

"I am sorry, for the trouble I've caused you, Grandmother. We have walked long and far, with nothing to eat. Bandits robbed us of what little we had and left us to live or die as we would."

The old woman gave them a knowing look-over. "What, a pair of strong boys with swords, and you let yourselves be taken by bandits?"

Halitor blushed and stammered, but Melly glanced down and it seemed to Halitor that she was remembering that she was supposed to be a boy.

"They came upon us when we were, ah, temporarily separated. I'd left my sword off, and they took me at, ah, a disadvantage." She did a pretty good imitation of a boy not wanting to tell an old woman he'd been behind a tree relieving himself. "Hal here gave them what they wanted, to save my life. He's my brother," she added. Despite both having hair in shades of brown, they looked nothing alike, but the woman didn't challenge the claim. "When they let me go, we chased them to try to get our food and money back, but they had horses and fled too fast for us to follow."

"Why didn't they take your swords?" the old woman wanted to know.

Melly hesitated a moment, and Halitor jumped in with the best answer he could think of. "It was pretty near dark, and I'd set mine off with Mel—uh, Melvern's sword." He stuttered a bit as he made up a boy's name for Melly. "I think they didn't see them."

The crone looked from one to another, and Halitor had a feeling that their lies had been pointless. She looked like the sort who knew everything under the sun, including that Melly was a girl and that they'd never had any money in the first place. He wished they'd hidden their swords, which as peasant lads they shouldn't even have had.

That was the last thought Halitor had for some time, because while he was talking, the woman filled two bowls with the stew that bubbled so enticingly over the fire. She handed one to each of them and they sat on the floor near the flames and thought about nothing but eating as she filled and refilled their bowls.

By the time they finished and Melly thanked her, it was growing late, and the light in the hut was dim.

"Ye boys go to the barn now and throw down some hay for me cows. Save me old bones the climb to the loft. Then yens can bed down in the hay if yens want."

Melly and Halitor exchanged looks. Then Halitor followed her out the door, with no idea what she had hoped he would understand from her look. For his part, he had been trying to say, "I don't think it's entirely safe to stay around here, but I'm really too tired to care," which is a lot to say with a single look.

Once outside, Melly stretched and gave an immense yawn. "We can't stay. It's not safe," she whispered.

"We have to do the hay," Halitor said. "We took the food." The Guide was extremely clear about that sort of thing, whatever danger the Hero might fear.

"Yes, I see that," Melly agreed, though she still frowned. "Anyway, a little more darkness would be good before we take to the road." It was a great deal lighter outside than it had been in the hut, which had but one small window. "But the woman—" Melly didn't finish the thought. Instead, she said, "'Melvern'? You couldn't give me a better name than that?"

Halitor shrugged. "I had to say something fast. I ought to know my brother's name."

Melly shrugged. "I don't suppose it matters." She yawned. "I'm awfully tired. Being awakened early by dragons and walking all day without breakfast wears a body out."

Halitor nodded, yawning as well. "I don't feel like I could go on." Melly's unfinished sentence nibbled at the back of his mind, but the need for sleep drove everything else away.

"We'll feed the animals and rest a bit, and leave well before dawn," she decided.

A few minutes later, they were lying on a pile of musty hay, and Halitor was snoring lightly.

Halitor woke up knowing something was wrong. He knew that because a grey and dismal daylight filled the loft, and because his head pounded and his mouth felt full of cotton, and especially because someone was standing over him tickling his throat with a sword.

It was his own sword, and the man who wielded it was demanding, "Where have you hidden your money? Tell me quick or I'll turn you into pig food."

Everyone knew pigs would eat anything, even Heroes. Halitor opened his mouth to say they didn't have any money. Then, for maybe the first time in his life, he thought through a bit of tricky reasoning and closed his mouth again. From across the loft, Melly spoke up.

"Put down our swords, scum, and we'll maybe think about telling you. Or," her voice trailed off as though she'd been distracted by a thought.

"Or what, boy? You'll beat me up? Bite my kneecap?" Guffaws from a number of men suggested the lout guarding her was even larger and less civil than the one who threatened

56

Halitor. It also told him that there were more than just the two swordsmen in the loft with them. He tried to turn his head to look, but the sword pressed a little harder on his throat.

"Don't move, carrion."

Halitor didn't like that name at all. He knew what carrion was. Carrion was the dead animals the vultures ate.

He held very still and waited for Melly to get them out of this one.

CHAPTER 6: ESCAPE!

"You're the Hero," Melly said. "You get us out of this."

They sat on the straw, bound back to back. The men had left the loft, taking the youngsters' packs and swords with them. Rain pounded on the roof, here and there leaking through to drip on the hay, and on Halitor's head. The noise of the rain made it impossible to tell if the men were still in the barn or waited nearby.

Halitor mumbled something.

"What?" Melly asked.

He gulped. "You're the one with ideas. I'm just, just," he tugged at his bonds for the hundredth time, and for the hundredth time gave up. "I'm just Halitor the Hapless." He said it with all the bitterness of crushed hopes. He'd only just started to think he might really manage to become a Hero, and now this happened.

Maybe he also said it in hopes that Melly would tell him he wasn't all that bad. Instead, she said, "As long as you think like that you will be hapless! What kind of Hero waits around for other people to solve his problems? And a girl, at that."

"Hush!" Halitor warned. "Least said about that the better. Anyway, maybe we should think, not argue."

He could feel her sigh.

"Well, that's sense, anyway." Her tone was grudging, but she stopped griping. They sat for a long time without speaking. Halitor tried to have an idea. He tried so hard his hair hurt.

"We have to get free of this rope," he said at last.

"I know that! How?"

"Well. Um, do you see anything rough or sharp on your side?"

She looked around. He could feel the bonds shift as she peered around as much of the loft as she could see. He did the same, without finding anything.

"Maybe…"

"What?" Halitor felt the rope shift a little more as Melly leaned hard to one side.

"There's a nail. An old rusty one that might be rough enough to wear through the rope if we can rub it back and forth over it. But how do we get there, tied like we are?"

"They didn't tie our feet," Halitor said. "We just have to work together."

Their struggles to rise and move would have made a watcher laugh. Even Halitor and Melly giggled some, until they remembered that when the ruffians found they had nothing worth stealing, they would most likely come back and kill them, or sell them as slaves, which was probably why they hadn't been killed before they even awoke. The thought sobered them and focused their minds on escape.

They made it to their feet at last, and Melly walked forward while Halitor hopped backwards, across the floor to the nail. Halitor concentrated and managed not to fall or even to step on Melly. If she noticed, she didn't say so. When they reached the wall, they turned so that both, craning their necks, could see the nail.

The nail was head high. No matter what they did, they couldn't reach their ropes up to it. They tried all sorts of maneuvers, and it simply couldn't be done. Even if they could reach it, Halitor doubted that the nail would saw through their ropes in anything less than a week.

They also noticed that their struggles had loosened the ropes around them. All Halitor's pulling against them while they sat had produced no effect, but the squirming and twisting and wriggling they'd done to stand up and cross the room had shifted them. The ropes had shifted, and Halitor caught his breath. Could they wriggle out of their bonds?

The bandits had tied them by looping a rope around both torsos, arms and all, half a dozen times, then tying it off. They hadn't been very careful. Two such young, skinny boys couldn't be much of a problem, right? They'd made lots of jokes about that, and Halitor had fumed at being dismissed as weak and helpless.

Now he thought maybe the joke was on the bandits.

"Melly?" he whispered. "I think there's a little slack in these ropes now."

She moved a bit, and the ropes slid a little more. "Is the knot coming loose?"

"I don't think so. I think when they tied us up, we were kind of slumped, and now we're standing and it makes us skinnier, and there's a little slack. And maybe," he hesitated and turned red, even though she couldn't see him. "Maybe if we squeeze together, and blow out all our air—"

She finished for him. "We can slide out of the ropes!" She tried an experimental wriggle. "I think it might have to be you," she said. Her voice sounded funny. "The ropes run both above and below my, uh..." She hesitated. It seemed even Melly could be embarrassed about some things.

"Right," Halitor said hastily. He wriggled a little, experimenting in his turn.

After some trial and error, they found that they could make the ropes slide a tiny bit at a time down his torso. Halitor thought it took forever. He was sure the bandits would come back and find them, and they had to stop sometimes because their heads swam from the effort and the effects of whatever the old witch had given them in their stew.

After what seemed like a hundred years, the rope slid below Halitor's elbows, and then it all came loose in a hurry. He could move his arms to the front, pull them up out of the rope loops, and they were free. The rope dropped to the floor and Melly stepped out of the coils.

Halitor went to the window. The day was getting old. They must have slept all night and half the day before the bandits came. No wonder his head felt funny. He couldn't see anyone about. Had they all gone?

"Where are they?" he whispered, though the rain still drummed on the roof, covering all their noise.

"Not down below in the barn," she said, "or

61

they'd have heard us by now."

"If we wait until dark we could just walk away and they'd never see us," he said.

"And what if they come back for us before then? We would be well and truly trapped up here. Besides," Melly added, "I want my sword back. And my blanket, if I can get it, and some food wouldn't hurt. But definitely my sword."

"How are you going to do that?" Halitor argued. "There are six of them to two of us, and they have our weapons. We'd do better just to run as fast and as far as we can before they know we're gone."

"You can do as you like, of course," Melly said, sounding indifferent. "I'm getting my sword back."

Halitor knew he didn't have a choice. It wasn't just that he never could resist Melly. A Hero couldn't leave a girl to do something like that alone. He heaved up a sigh from the ends of his toes. "What's your plan?"

Melly didn't answer for a moment. If he hadn't known better, Halitor might have thought she didn't have a plan, that she was making one up right then. That couldn't be true, because Melly always had a plan.

"Well," she said, "let's start by getting out of here." She led the way to the ladder. They'd already made enough noise to wake the dead, had there been anyone in the barn to hear, but they still moved quietly, and when Melly reached the floor she stepped quickly behind a partition out of sight of the door.

Halitor did the same, and as he had neither sword, pack, nor blanket-cloak to trip him up, managed to do it silently.

His little triumph was wasted. There was no one to hear—or rather, to not hear. The barn was as empty as they had expected. They heard only the sounds of animals eating and the rain on the roof.

Melly led the way to the back of the building, farther from the house, and Halitor hoped she had seen the wisdom of just slipping away, glad to be alive. A small door led out to the yard. Rain still pounded down, and Halitor didn't want to go out. He didn't want to stay in the barn and wait for the bandits to come back, either. He followed her out into the rain.

A few steps carried them into the forest, where it was already night. Halitor bumped into Melly, who had stopped and turned.

"We'll find a sheltered spot and wait for them to all go to sleep." She was already beginning to shiver, her clothes and hair wet from the dash through the rain, which was now coming down in sheets.

"What if they go to the barn to check on us?" Halitor whispered, while he led her into a sheltered spot under the low-sweeping branches of a fir tree.

"Listen to them. Do they sound like folk who are going to check on their captives?" Melly spoke with scorn, and Halitor listened to the sounds they could hear drifting from the hut, now that they were out of the echoing barn.

He knew that kind of singing. That was the kind of singing soldiers had done at the Drunken Bard. Soldiers who had spent a long evening trying to forget that they were soldiers.

63

He listened some more. He knew that song. His mother had once washed his mouth out with soap for singing it. He'd learned it from the peddler who came to their village every spring. The one who had known better than to hire young Halitor, but not better than to teach him ribald songs.

"We'd better make ourselves comfy," he said. "It usually takes an hour or two to get from that song to sleeping on the table." He saw her plan now, such as it was. If the men were drinking— and that song meant drinking—it might work. He wrapped them both in a dusty horse-blanket he'd thought to grab from a hook near the door as they'd gone out.

Would the old woman be drinking too?

Thoughts like that kept Halitor from getting too comfortable, which was good. He didn't want to sleep, but whatever the old witch had put in the stew still made him groggy, when he stopped to notice. He was also hungry again, as well as wet and cold, so he stayed awake in spite of magic potions or sleep spells.

Melly led the way in their silent return across the dark farmyard. A light still burned in the hut, but all had been silent for a long time.

"I just wish I knew what that old woman was up to," Halitor whispered when they started out. Melly shrugged, and he followed her, moving without sound and wishing there were bushes or trees to hide behind. There was only the darkness, the rain, and knowing that anyone in the hut would be night-blind with the lantern light. But what of someone left outside? They might have posted a guard.

He had to comfort himself with the thought that no one had stopped them when they left the barn. Surely if there had been a guard, he'd have spotted them then. And no one had left the hut since. The rain helped. No bandit would want to wait around outside in the wet. And the rain made a lot of noise. It would cover any little sounds they might make.

Melly reached the window, sidling along the wall toward it and then dropping into a crouch below the opening. Not making a sound, she raised herself until her eyes topped the sill, then held still. The window was only a rough hole in the wall, so there was nothing between her and whatever was inside.

At last she dropped down and crept back to Halitor.

"They sleep," she whispered with barely a sound. "Our things are on the table, as though they'd been studying them, or gambling for them." She pushed her dripping hair out of her eyes.

"Even our swords?"

"Yes." She hesitated. "The two who used them against us sleep there, with their hands on the hilts."

Halitor wanted to restart the argument for leaving without their weapons, but he knew it would get him nowhere and just make a noise. Then she added, "There's a loaf of bread on the table, too," and he followed her lead without further complaint, waiting silently beside her while she reached through the opening and pulled out one item after another, starting with

65

their packs. He stowed everything, including the bread, and they put the packs on before Melly tried for the swords. She stretched her full length, leaning in the opening, but sank back empty-handed.

"I can't reach. You'll have to do it."

They traded places and Halitor peered over the sill. Sure enough, the bandits slept and snored, scattered about the room as though they had fallen asleep in the middle of their drunken revelries. The two at the table lay face down, outstretched hands on the hilts of the two swords. It reminded him of stories he'd heard, where an enchantment put everyone to sleep as soon as someone touched some magical object. Of course, they'd handled the swords earlier without harm, but the thought made him look around for the old woman. She was nowhere to be seen. He glanced back at Melly, who watched him, looking more worried than he'd ever seen her.

"Don't watch me," he hissed. "Watch our backs!" Both of them were shaking with the cold, and they needed to get moving, but he wouldn't be hurried.

She glared, then nodded and turned to survey the yard. He reached through the window with both hands, taking great care to make no sound. He thought that it might be best to get both swords at once, in case the men woke up when the weapons moved.

To Halitor's amazement, his plan worked. The swords slid free, and he lifted them carefully through the window. He was just turning to hand one to Melly when a voice cackled from the darkness.

"So you are wandering, my children? You never were their prisoners, you know." She raised a bony finger to point at the window, and turned to point it at them.

Halitor froze, with no idea what to do. He was too well brought-up to attack an old woman, even if he she was a witch who was about to put a spell on them.

Melly had no such scruples. She leaped forward, knocked the witch into the barnyard mud, and sprinted for the road. Halitor shook off his paralysis and caught up to her in three strides, miraculously neither dropping nor tripping on the swords.

As they ran they listened for sounds of pursuit, and heard nothing but their own rasping breaths. Then came a faint cackle that might have been an old witch's laughter.

At the sound, Halitor and Melly found they could run a little faster.

CHAPTER 7: DEALS WITH GIANTS

Halitor and Melly ran until they could run no more, stumbling and falling and getting up to run again. When they were too tired to run another step, they walked. They walked the rest of the night, worn out but unwilling to stop. When they paused, it seemed to them they could still hear the witch's cackle, and it drove them on.

When it grew light, they left the road and sought a safe place to hole up and sleep. If the bandits—or the witch, who seemed to be both with the bandits and yet not part of them—came looking, they wanted to be nowhere in sight. And though it had stopped raining, they wanted shelter in case it started again.

It was Halitor who found the cave, but they both studied it dubiously. The last cave Melly had entered had been the residence of a dragon, and though the creature had not performed exactly according to the Guide, they couldn't count on that sort of luck again.

It was quite a shallow cave, and showed no signs of habitation. It was really just a couple of huge rocks tilted together.

"It seems safe enough."

"Ye-es." Melly looked around and shrugged.

The cave was the only shelter, as the rising sun destroyed the shadows under the now-sparse trees. For the last few miles they had been walking between fields of low crops, so even sparse trees felt like shelter, but not shelter enough for sleeping. Not with so many people hunting them. They wanted to hide, though they also longed to stretch themselves in the sun and warm up. Nor had they forgotten the dragon. Sleeping in the open seemed a very bad idea.

Melly shrugged. "We have to rest. And I'm sure this is too far down in the valley for monsters to live in the caves. There are farms all around. We'll be fine."

Halitor wished she hadn't said that. Every time he thought they were safe something went wrong. Yet Melly was right; they could walk no further. They could barely stand. And the cave was the best hiding place around. He crawled into the shelter, Melly right behind him, and they tried to make themselves comfortable while they ate the loaf of bread they had taken along with their own goods. Halitor thought he should stay awake to guard them, but fell asleep thinking about it.

Halitor wasn't surprised to wake up and find that something was wrong. He was coming to expect it. In this case, something large was blocking the light that should have been streaming into their cave through the opening. And something smelled very, very bad. He was sure he knew that smell, and after a little thought he remembered. Once, he and Bovrell had rescued a Princess from a giant, up north of Hamran, in

Kargor. They'd gone right into its cave, and Halitor had nearly passed out from the smell.

Now Halitor breathed through his mouth and tried not to choke or gag or make any other noise. A glance showed him Melly was still asleep. He lay still and thought for a minute or two.

Did the giant know they were there? Was he blocking their escape on purpose, or was he just leaning against a convenient boulder for an afternoon rest? And did it matter, if they were to be poisoned either way?

Melly started to stir, her nose twitching and face wrinkling as the stench penetrated even her exhausted sleep. He had to do something or she'd make a noise, and then they'd really be in trouble.

He sat up cautiously, laid aside his blanket without a sound, and crawled to her side. The tiny scuffling noises he made went unheard. It was the giant's big backside that blocked their escape. His ears were a long way off.

Halitor laid a finger on Melly's lips as her eyes fluttered open. She understood at once, and asked her questions with a look and no words. He shifted and pointed to the vast fur-clad mass of flesh blocking the opening, and her eyes opened wider, but she still made no sound. Halitor admired someone who could take in all that and not squeak. Really, Melly was not like any girl he'd ever seen. The Princesses and Fair Maidens he and Bovrell had rescued had all done lots of shrieking and fainting, and the other kitchen wenches at the Drunken Bard were much given to giggling and squeaking.

70

Melly sat up and began to fold and stow her blanket, so Halitor did the same. There wasn't room in their cave to stand, but they could sit, and when their packs were ready, that's what they did. They sat, and they thought, or at least Halitor hoped they were thinking. After a bit, he noticed that there was more light in the cave than he would have expected with the entrance blocked.

He began to look about him, and saw that the light came from an opening at the back, up a narrow crack. He pointed, and they both crawled closer. Alas, the possibilities were limited. They could reach a hand out the opening, and fresher air came in, but there was no hope of escape that way. Halitor was testing to see if he could enlarge the hole when a sound made him stiffen. He flung his head up to listen, and banged it on the low stone roof.

The sound was as a distant rumbling, like thunder in the next valley. A moment later the rumbling gave way to a series of reports and explosions, so close he and Melly both flinched. Halitor thought a rockslide was coming to engulf them. Though that would take care of the giant, it seemed all too likely it would take care of them, too.

Then Halitor realized it was much worse than a rockslide. He could feel the warm gasses around his feet and ankles, and then the odor reached his nose. Whatever the giant had eaten, it didn't agree with him. If they had still been asleep on the ground, they might now be dead.

"We have to get out of here!" Melly gasped in his ear.

71

"How? Can you crawl out that hole?" He knew she couldn't, but if only she could!

Melly studied the hole, wiggled free a couple of loose bits, and he boosted her up. She struggled, but there was no way to fit more than an arm and shoulder out. He lowered her and they slumped against the wall in a half-crouch, keeping their faces as near the hole as they could.

"We are stuck." Melly sighed, as though it hurt her to admit it.

"Maybe he'll just up and leave?"

"Do you want to bet on it?"

They lapsed into silence once more. Gradually the noxious fumes dissipated, and they could sit again, easing their aching legs. Halitor began fingering the hilt of his sword.

A new sort of rumbling startled him out of his thoughts. After a tense moment, he recognized the sound, though it was louder than any he had ever heard. The giant was snoring.

Halitor took some comfort from that. Surely if the giant knew they were there and wanted to kill them, it wouldn't have gone to sleep. He thought some more, and an idea burst in on his ruminations.

In a whisper much quieter than the giant's snorts and rumblings Halitor said, "Let's poke him with a sword. Maybe he'll think it's a stick or a rock and go look for a more comfortable place to nap."

"And maybe," Melly protested, "he'll come in after us."

"He can't." Halitor sat up. "Look, he can maybe peer in—I'm not saying his head wouldn't fit. Or reach a hand in, maybe, but not both at the same time. And we have swords. If he sticks anything through that hole, we can cut it off."

It was the boldest and most bloodthirsty plan he had ever made. It felt good.

They crept into position. Melly readied herself on the opening's left, sword raised to hack off whatever presented itself for hacking. Halitor knelt in front of the hole, close enough to allow for easy poking, but out of the way of Melly's sword.

His first pokes were gentle. When the snoring didn't falter, he poked harder. It took a number of rather energetic prods before the rumbling snore ceased and the fleshy mass moved. A gap appeared around the vast posterior, and Halitor had hopes the giant would just get up and wander off. Instead, a hand appeared and fumbled blindly, as though searching for the pesky rock, stick or beast that jabbed it.

Halitor moved a little further back, and Melly took a firmer grip on her sword. There wasn't much room to swing, so they'd need to put all their strength into it if they had to start cutting off bits of giant.

The hand withdrew without exploring the cave. But the giant didn't move away. Unable to feel the prickly thing with its hand, it made a great lumbering turn, and a moment later a huge, red, and bewildered face appeared in the opening.

This was the point where they were supposed to attack.

Halitor didn't know why Melly didn't follow the plan. She never seemed to hesitate at much of anything. When Halitor looked at that great, round, red face he just couldn't do it. It looked so much like the face of old Perkin, the village idiot who spent every evening at the Drunken Bard, pickling what few brains he had. It was a face without hatred or desire to harm.

Halitor and Melly pressed against the cave's walls, not moving, and hoped to remain unseen.

The ox-like brown eyes blinked. The nostrils, each the size of Halitor's fist, with boogers to match, flared and twitched.

"Hullo?" The huge lips parted to let out the word, exposing a row of ill-cleaned, blunt teeth. "Anyone home? Oh, bother!" The giant paused. "How does that go again?" He muttered a bit to himself and tried it out. "Foof, um, fee fo? I smell—no, that's not it." The massive face screwed itself into a caricature of thought. "I've forgotten again."

Halitor felt a rush of fellow-feeling. Before he could stop himself, he said, "Can we help you?" He clapped a hand over his mouth and looked at Melly, but she had already reached out to pat the curly head.

"We'll take it as said," she offered, "if you'll just move a bit and let us out. Then you don't have to try to eat us, and we don't have to cut off your head."

More visible efforts at thought. Then the giant nodded.

Rather, he tried to nod. There wasn't room, so first he banged his head on the rock above, then mashed his face into the sandy floor, and came up sputtering. Halitor and Melly had to dodge flying bits of giant-spittle coated sand.

"I don't even like eating people," the giant said when he could speak again. "I want to be a vegetarian. But Mama says we're supposed to steal sheep and goats and eat them raw. She says there's no such thing as a vegetarian giant."

"Are there enough vegetables in the world to feed you?" Halitor asked before thinking. The giant didn't take offense.

"Oh, I like trees. Plenty of trees up on the mountain. But Mama sent me down here and told me to eat some sheep. I hate sheep. The wool gets stuck in my teeth."

"Well," urged Melly again, "why don't you move a bit so we can come out and help you?"

The head withdrew, and Melly started for the opening. Halitor grabbed her. "Are you mad? What if he's lying? As soon as you step out there, he'll have you! At least we're safe in here!"

"Safe, and getting nowhere. Can't you tell when someone is speaking the truth?"

After that, there was nothing to do but go first, so he did.

Halitor, despite his momentary sympathy for the giant who couldn't seem to do anything right, pretty much expected to be eaten the moment he crawled out, before he could stand up and use his sword. He didn't realize that he was being brave again. He thought that brave people were never scared, whereas the truth is that people who are never scared have no need of courage.

Halitor stood up, sword in hand, and looked at the giant. It—he—didn't appear to be planning on eating anyone. He sat a few yards away, his head in his giant hands. Halitor knew that posture, because he'd sat that way himself all too often. The giant was unhappy, discouraged, and about to start crying.

Melly crawled out and stood next to him. No one said anything for a while.

Then the giant looked up. He was just as ugly and stupid-looking as they had thought, but also very young and not all that big, for a giant. He wasn't more than twice the size of Halitor, who was a well-grown young man when not half-starved.

"I'm no good," the giant said. "I can't even eat two little humans."

"Perhaps that's because you aren't meant to," Melly said. "Who says you have to eat people?"

"Mama. She's been reading a book that says that's what we do. And she seems willing enough."

Halitor felt the weight of that answer. Hadn't his own mother pushed him from task to task and master to master, insisting he find a career? And he had never been able to say no. And with a book to back her up—a book like the Guide? Now he thought about it, the *Hero's Guide* said that giants ate people. Could it be wrong? He felt a wave of confusion that nearly knocked him down.

Melly suffered from no such confusion, having no experience with either overbearing mothers or the Guide. "Nonsense! If you don't want to eat people—or sheep—you don't have to. You aren't a baby anymore, uh—what's your name?"

"Rawgool."

"Well, Rawgool, you look grown up to me. You don't have to do what your mother says."

Rawgool and Halitor both stared at her. It had never occurred to Halitor that you could grow up and just stop doing whatever your mother said. Of course, he hadn't seen his mother since he was thirteen, so maybe that was why. Still, what did Melly really know? She'd said she had no mother.

"Mama says I'm too stupid to live alone, so I have to stay with her and let her tell me what to do. And I'm only thirty-five. She says a giant isn't grown up until he's fifty or so."

"Nonsense," Melly said again. "And you never will grow up if you let her boss you around all your life." She didn't say if she thought he was stupid.

Halitor, in addition to all his other miseries, had been dreading the day when he'd have to go home and tell his Ma and Da he'd failed again. For the first time, it occurred to him that maybe he didn't have to go back to them. That he could arrange his own life and go where he wanted. The thought made him dizzy.

Rawgool also looked like it was a new and happy thought. Then his face fell.

"I don't think I know how," he began.

"You can find the forest, can't you?"

"I suppose so."

Halitor rolled his eyes. Anyone could find the forest. It was everywhere. Maybe this giant really was too stupid to live alone.

"Then what else do you need?" Melly asked.

"I don't know."

That stopped even Melly. Could a giant live

77

on just trees? With maybe some broccoli thrown in? None of them knew. And what about clothes? If he wouldn't kill and eat animals, where would he get the skins to cover his giant body? Surely even a giant got cold in winter. Then Melly smiled.

"I know! You come along with us for a bit. We'll help you discover what you need."

"That sounds nice," said Rawgool. "But," his face wrinkled with worry, "what can I do for you? Mama always says you have to help those who help you. That's why I had to do what she said."

"What did you do for her?" Halitor asked, curious as to what chores a young giant might have to perform.

"Moved rocks. Lots of rocks."

"That doesn't sound like fun." Though it wasn't so much worse than some of what Halitor had done over the years.

"No, it doesn't," Melly broke in. "And we don't need rocks moved. But I think you can help just by being with us. We've had a spot of trouble with ogres and bandits and the like. I don't think they'd bother us with you along."

"I don't know how to fight."

"You don't have to. Just look big and yell if they get too close."

Rawgool brightened. "I could do that."

"Yes," Melly said. "You'd be our guard."

Halitor gulped once to get rid of his last lingering fear of the giant, and then gulped again to hide a sudden pang of jealousy. He was Melly's guard! Perhaps he hadn't been very good at it, but they were still alive and free.

Though he had to admit that if they were, it was as much her doing as his.

He swallowed one more time, smiled at Rawgool and said, "That would be helpful."

After all, *The Hero's Guide to Battles, Rescues and the Slaying of Monsters* did say that a Hero should be gracious and generous in victory.

CHAPTER 8: BANDITS AGAIN!

The three travelers started on, not waiting now for night to give them cover. Halitor didn't think anyone would bother them, not with a giant as one of their party. The witch might be harder to intimidate, but he didn't suppose she would or could travel so far from her cottage. They had run a long way the previous night. Even if she wanted to follow, how could an old woman catch up with them?

They traveled for three days without any incident, and without being rained on, either. Halitor began to feel more cheerful, and to think perhaps they could reach Melly's home without further trouble. He even began to enjoy the journey, even though he was always hungry.

Now and again Rawgool ate a branch pulled from a young oak or a small fir, and Melly convinced him to try broccoli.

"I like it," he said in a surprised tone. "It looks like little green trees, and it tastes good."

Halitor still worried that Rawgool might need meat to be strong. He and Melly did. They could, and did, eat the broccoli that Melly plucked from the fields. Halitor hated broccoli. He didn't consider it stealing to take the vegetable, because who would want broccoli anyway? He ate it because he was hungry, but he didn't like it, and it didn't keep his stomach filled for long.

Halitor also worried about the giant's smell, which had so nearly overcome them in the cave, but out in the open air it seemed insignificant, and indeed as Rawgool ate more trees, and none of the sheep—or other meats—his Mama had forced on him, his gas got much better.

After making camp each night Halitor set snares, but he didn't catch anything until the second evening, when he managed to frighten a fox from its kill. He took the rabbit back to camp.

"Half for you, Rawgool, and half for Melly and me."

Rawgool shook his big head. "I don't want any."

"Surely you need to eat some meat," Halitor protested. "You can't possibly fill up on just trees."

Rawgool broke a branch from a nearby oak and nibbled a few twigs. "I feel fine. You two, though," he said, looking the humans over, "you two I think need to eat more."

Halitor and Melly looked at each other, considering the ragged clothes that hung loose about them. Rawgool was right, they needed all the food they could get, and the rabbit would be a nice addition to their skimpy diet. If he wasn't smart, Rawgool was observant.

Their trip got better after they came upon a young man hunting in the forest the next morning. When he saw Rawgool, he dropped his bow and fled. Melly leapt on the bow, though Halitor felt sorry for the boy, who would have to explain to someone how he had lost it. Besides, Halitor knew he was a lousy shot, so it wouldn't do them much good to have a bow.

Melly, as it turned out, was a very good shot. It occurred to Halitor to wonder how a kitchen wench, or even a wine merchant's daughter, had learned to shoot so well, but he was too grateful for her hunting success to ask questions. Now they had meat for every meal, and Halitor started tanning the hides. He didn't do it well, because he'd only been apprenticed to the tanner for three weeks. But Rawgool would need more skins, with winter coming. So would they, if they didn't reach Melly's home soon.

By the third day, they relaxed enough to travel on the road itself. They gave cheerful greetings to all they met, though most were running away too fast to return the greetings. Rawgool seemed to make other travelers uncomfortable, though Halitor thought that if the people weren't so silly they'd know that he was friendly, because he was traveling with a pair of humans and not eating them even a little bit. People didn't seem to think of that. For some reason, that filled them all with high spirits, so that in the afternoon they sang as they walked.

Halitor was trying to teach Rawgool the words to "A Hero Went a-Heroing," when he looked ahead and fell silent. Melly looked at him when he stopped singing, then followed his gaze. Her lips drew into a tight line and her hand strayed to her sword hilt.

An old woman waited for them in the road. When they were some twenty paces away, and could see that it was indeed the old woman, the witch, they halted. After a moment, Melly spoke while Halitor continued to gape.

"Good afternoon, Grandmother. I fear we must apologize for leaving without thanking you for your hospitality." Halitor knew that it was always best to be polite to a witch, but he didn't think he could be as polite as Melly was. He wanted to yell at the old woman for betraying them to the bandits. And Melly hadn't just left without thanking the woman. She'd knocked her into the mud, a fact he didn't think the old witch would soon forget. Still, a pretense of manners couldn't hurt.

No one else was on the road, just the three of them and the old woman.

They stood face to face with the witch who had magicked Melly and Halitor into the hands of the bandits, and none of them moved. This was a difficult situation for a Hero. On the one hand, a witch could do a lot of harm if not prevented. On the other, a Hero couldn't attack an old woman. He wasn't even allowed to be rude to her. Even if it wasn't a bad idea to be rude to someone who could put you to sleep and maybe turn you into something nasty, the Guide was very clear on the treatment of women and elders. Did that include witches?

Melly seemed to know what to do. She kept right on talking, her tone polite, though she did seem to be rewriting history as she spoke.

"You see, Grandmother, we didn't care for the company you keep. I'm sure you had no idea, but those fellows were bandits, and thought to steal what little we poor travelers had. Had we let them, I greatly fear they would next have turned their weapons on you."

Melly had to stop then to draw breath, and the witch at once began to speak in a weak, low tone that forced them to listen closely, even to come a few steps nearer.

"My child, you wrong an old woman who only wished to help hungry and benighted younglings." She seemed as willing as Melly to ignore what had been said and done beneath the window, but her voice was barely audible.

Despite themselves, Melly and Halitor leaned a little closer to hear what she said. The words went on and on. Halitor could no longer tell what she was saying, and knew only that he must hold still and listen. He began to sway.

Just before Halitor lost himself completely in the murmuring voice, a loud noise broke the spell. It was the sound of falling trees or an erupting mountain, and it jarred him from the trance the witch had woven about them. A wave of choking gasses followed the noise, destroying the last remnants of the spell. The stink passed, pushed toward the witch by a light breeze. Halitor and Melly both shook off the enchantment as the witch fled, and turned to Rawgool.

"I'm sorry," the giant muttered, red-faced. "I did try to wait until you were finished, but it went on a long time and I couldn't hear what she said—" He broke off when they began to laugh.

Halitor glanced down the road and saw the witch had gone, whether fleeing the gas attack or dismayed by the failure of her spell, he hoped he'd never need to know.

"Oh, my! Rawgool!" Melly was gasping. "I thought you'd got over that! But," she added quickly as he turned still redder, "you couldn't have done it at a better time."

"I couldn't?"

"No! Didn't you do it on purpose, to break the spell?"

"Spell?"

Melly and Halitor stopped laughing and looked at him. "Couldn't you feel the spell she was weaving? She'd caught our minds, and was witching us to her will. I'd almost forgotten who I was and why we were here when you…woke us up."

The giant shook his head.

"You didn't feel the magic?" Melly asked again.

He shook his head again. "Giants don't use magic. I couldn't hear what she was saying," Rawgool said. "And I got tired of waiting. And I ate all those cabbages last night, and they made my tummy go funny."

Melly said, "I suppose she didn't know her spell was only good on humans. Maybe giants don't use magic because magic doesn't work on giants. Or maybe she didn't realize you were with us, and left you out of her weaving. Either way, you saved us."

They began walking again. Halitor kept a sharp lookout for the witch—or her bandit minions. Though they'd moved fast, if the bandits had horses, they could have moved still faster. In fact, that must have been how the old woman had gotten ahead of them. He'd seen no horses at her cottage, but she must have ridden, and where else would she get a horse than from the bandits?

They rounded a curve in the road and Halitor discovered he was right.

"Ow!" Rawgool was the first to know about the ambush. An arrow struck his shin, bruising the leg through his heavy boot. It was just enough warning. The two humans dove for cover behind a large rock, Rawgool a step behind them.

Melly strung her bow grimly. She had three arrows. That was not enough, even though she would doubtless score with each shot. When the three bolts were fired, Halitor thought, he could be a Hero at last, and sell his life dearly in protecting her. If she'd let herself be protected.

Halitor had reckoned without Rawgool. The giant carried no weapons, since he didn't like hurting and killing even small animals, and Halitor had come to think of him as a form of intimidation. And the bandits had fired on them despite the giant.

Halitor hadn't counted on the giant's loyalty. He disliked killing small furry animals with big eyes, but he disliked still more people who shot arrows at him and his friends. Halitor and Melly had made Rawgool feel capable for the first time in his life, and when the giant had agreed to protect them, it was an agreement he took more seriously than they did.

Picking up a stone in each fist, Rawgool peered from behind the boulder and flung first one and then the other at the approaching bandits. He hit what he aimed for. Two men fell in the road, and it didn't look like they would be getting up.

Melly paused just before firing, looked at

Rawgool, and saved her arrows. The giant rained stones on the enemy. Halitor sheathed his sword so he could scramble about and gather ammunition for the giant. The flurry of fist-sized stones—and a giant's fist is large—soon discouraged the attackers. In a minute they were retreating in a disorganized hurry.

Unfortunately, the bandits didn't take themselves off somewhere to find other victims. They drew back a safe distance, out of range of rock or arrow, and bunched up, as though planning their next move.

Melly left Halitor and Rawgool to keep watch and mock the bandits, while she scrambled about to collect all the arrows she could find.

A coarse-voiced man stood up and shouted, "Give up now while you're still in one piece!"

"We'd never surrender to low-down bullies like you," Halitor yelled back. "I hope the witch turns you all into frogs for failing to capture us."

"You couldn't catch a cold," Rawgool added. To Halitor, he said, "that's what Ma always said when I'd come back from a hunt without anything."

Melly had collected a dozen or more arrows, and the bandits had resorted to coarse language, when Halitor said, "Uh-oh."

Melly hurried to look where he was looking. "Uh-oh what?"

"I think they're splitting up. This boulder only protects us from in front. What if they get behind us?" The bandits had stopped shouting and were moving about, so it was hard to keep track of them all.

With just three of them—and Halitor had no

weapon but his sword, good only at close range—they couldn't meet attacks from several sides at once. And if the enemy got far enough around the sides, they could just sit back and pick them off with arrows.

Halitor studied their surroundings. Could they beat a retreat before they were flanked? If they moved out from their shelter, they'd be shot. The bandits weren't that far away, plenty close enough now for arrows.

Then something unexpected happened.

Halitor had an idea.

Gathering a pile of rocks of a size he could manage, he explained. "Melly, you take the front. If they show themselves, shoot someone. Rawgool, that group on the right is yours." He'd noticed that Rawgool threw equally well with either hand, so it would be easier for him to defend that side. "When you see anyone, throw everything you can, and hit them." He suspected Rawgool hadn't liked seeing the two men he had maybe killed, and hadn't tried so hard to hit them after that.

Halitor saved the left flank for himself, because the enemy would draw closest there before being exposed. His rocks wouldn't fly as far or hit as hard as the giant's, but at close enough range they would hurt.

"If anyone's group breaks or makes an open-ing, yell and we can all run that way. Into the hills, up the road—I don't care. We just have to get out of this trap."

He was too busy piling rocks and finding the best firing position to realize that, for the first time since they had met, Melly didn't argue with him. She took up her post, put an arrow to the string, and did what she was told.

Then they waited. Halitor wasn't surprised to feel his knees shaking. You couldn't expect a failed Hero to be brave. He leaned against the boulder to steady himself and went on waiting. He hadn't known that waiting for an attack would be so hard, maybe worse than fighting.

Then it got even harder. Behind him, he heard Melly's bowstring twang, and grunts and scrabbling noises as Rawgool began to throw rocks and grab for more. He wanted to turn and watch them, but if he did, they'd be lost for sure. His job was the left flank, and he had to guard it and trust his friends.

A row of boulders about thirty paces out blocked his view of approaching bandits. One small gap revealed the low brush beyond. Trees were sparse, but rocks were large and plentiful and provided too much cover.

There! He spotted movement in the brush beyond the boulders. Halitor clutched his stones more tightly, then made himself relax. He'd throw no better if he wore himself out beforehand with his clutching.

Another hint of movement, and he decided to let them know he was watching. He threw, and was rewarded by a string of curses. He responded with a mocking reference to big babies who cried over little bumps, though he knew that his stones could do no real harm at such a distance. They might not even hurt enough to slow them down. And now they would be more careful.

It was time to get out of there. Halitor risked a

glance around, in time to see Rawgool lower his hands and peer about as though he'd run out of targets. Melly wasn't firing either.

"Rawgool!" Halitor hissed. "Throw everything you've got over on this side. Then let's run!"

Rawgool took a moment to make the change, but Melly caught on and turned quickly, managing to get an arrow into a careless bandit.

"You run! I follow," Rawgool grunted as he flung his missiles at anything that moved. Thinking of the giant's long legs and unerring aim, Halitor and Melly took his advice. Making one last check for lurking assailants, they broke for the woods on the right side. Bandits felled by Rawgool's stones littered the ground, and they dodged around them in case any were shamming. None jumped up to grab at them. If any were alive, they must have decided it was safer to keep on playing dead.

Rawgool made no effort to dodge the fallen bandits when he crossed the open ground a moment later. He just stepped on whatever lay in his way. He caught up to the other two and grabbed up one on each side. Tucking them under his arms, he sped up. Even burdened with a weight nearly equal to his own, he ran faster than the two humans could have over the rough ground.

When the giant, panting and breathless at last, let them down far from the battle, Melly gasped, "If I'd known you could run like that, I'd have had you take us off right away, and we wouldn't have had to kill any of them!"

"The fight was fun," Rawgool said.

Halitor looked at him. "I thought you didn't like hurting animals."

"Animals are nice," the giant said. "Bandits are bad." He reached down and plucked an arrow from his right leg. He gave it a disgusted look and tossed it aside.

"Oh!" Melly cried. "You're hurt."

"Not much. Giants have thick skin."

They looked, and saw Rawgool was right. Where he'd pulled out the arrow, a small trickle of blood ran down his leg, but Halitor had worse from a tree branch that had torn his arm during their wild flight.

"Huh," said Melly, seeing Halitor's blood. She tore a strip off his shirt and tied up the wound. Rawgool's wound she washed out, and decided it needed no bandages. That was a good thing, as it would have taken Halitor's whole shirt to make a bandage big enough to tie around the massive leg.

Rawgool held up a hand to stop her fussing over his wound, and cupped the other behind one ear.

"I think we better go now. Someone's coming. Maybe them?"

Halitor could hear nothing, but he didn't argue. Rawgool might not know much about the wider world of humans, but at some things he was better than Halitor or even, disloyal though it felt to think it, than Melly. His big ears heard more than they did, and Halitor envied the giant his strength. Reminding himself that what mattered was that they were alive, Halitor hitched his pack and sword more comfortably into place, and led off into the forest.

CHAPTER 9: MELLY GOES HOME

The three companions moved through the forest as quickly and quietly as they could, but it wasn't easy. If they wanted to be quiet, they had to pick their way carefully to avoid breaking branches and starting small rockslides. And if they wanted to be quick…Halitor thought they could only do that if they moved back down to the valley floor, because the hillside was a mess.

To stay hidden, they had climbed fairly high up the slopes, where the thicker forest offered cover. There were no paths, so they had to climb over and under fallen trees, and constantly detour around thick brush and sudden gullies that they couldn't climb through. It was slow going, and Halitor and Melly both accumulated a lot of scratches, and their clothes fared badly. Rawgool could have pushed through faster, but it would have made a great deal of noise, and left a trail the bandits could follow with their eyes closed.

They were all dismayed to find that the bandits had not given up, as ordinary bandits would when the quarry fought back and got away.

"They must be angry we hurt so many of

them," Halitor suggested. "They want revenge."

"Or," Melly began.

When she didn't go on, Halitor asked, "Or what?"

"I was thinking of, of her. But—oh, never mind. Let's keep moving."

Halitor wondered for a few minutes just what Melly was thinking about the witch, but the effort of keeping up with Rawgool soon drove everything else from his mind. It was an hour later before he remembered to ask, "Do you think the witch is part of the bandit crew?"

"I think she finds them useful."

It took Halitor another gully and three thickets to work that out. When he did, it gave him another question. "What is she up to? Bandits want to rob everyone, but what do old witches want with stray travelers? And why do any of them want us enough to chase us for four days? We don't have any money, or even any food!"

"It almost seems personal, doesn't it?" Melly's answer confused Halitor. What under the Ice Castle did that mean? That the witch held a grudge? He stopped trying to think and concentrated on not falling into ravines or cracking his skull on low-hanging branches.

By dusk they had circled around two villages and were drawing near to Alcedor, by far the largest settlement in the valley—or in any other valley that Halitor had seen.

There had been no sign of pursuit for some time, but Melly insisted they avoid people and stay off the road, in case the outlaws were lying in wait for them.

"With her behind them, and some of their people dead, they won't give up so easily," Melly said. "It doesn't matter that we've nothing worth stealing. It never was about money, or even slaves." Then she clamped her mouth shut and wouldn't say anything more.

Halitor didn't think she sounded much like a kitchen wench now. She sounded like someone who understood bandits and battles. He reminded himself that she had been taken captive by bandits once. Someone like Melly could have learned a lot from that experience.

Worse, he thought she was right. And if the bandits were after revenge, not loot, he and Melly were in a world of trouble.

It was nearing dark and they had drawn close to Alcedor. Now there were paths in the mountains, most leading down to the road or straight on to the city. It was the biggest place Halitor had ever seen.

"Of course it's big," Melly responded to his exclamations, without taking her own eyes from the walled settlement. "It's the capitol of Garan. Haven't you ever been there? I thought you and that moron went everywhere."

"Bovrell wouldn't come here. He said it was too far north, and not really much of a place anyway and, oh, what was the other thing? Oh, right—he said there weren't any Princesses there, so there was nothing for a Hero to do."

"Well!" Melly huffed.

"I think he had some reason to stay away," Halitor mused. "I used to think it was the cold, but we aren't really that far north. And it's certainly big enough. So he must have been making up excuses."

"I'm sure he was," Melly sniffed. "Probably he was hiding from debt collectors." She led the way to a rock outcrop with a good view of the city and the valley. All three sat down and considered the landscape. Halitor wanted to go down and find a meal and a bed. Despite hunger and fatigue Melly and Rawgool didn't agree.

"I don't think they'd like a giant down there," Rawgool said, and Halitor had to agree. Everywhere he'd ever been, people and giants were supposed to be enemies, and judging by the reactions they'd gotten on the road, the people around Alcedor agreed. So he understood why Rawgool didn't want to go down to the settled areas.

Melly's hesitation Halitor couldn't fathom. Surely she, too, was tired and hungry. She was a girl, by all the gods! Girls were supposed to be soft and to need protecting and nice beds to sleep in—though Halitor had to admit that the *Hero's Guide* had clearly not had Melly in mind when it described females. Perhaps that was because it concerned itself only with Princesses and Fair Maidens, not kitchen wenches.

Though if he let himself think of it, which he usually didn't, Halitor thought Melly was a fair-enough maiden. But she was no Princess. She'd been very clear about that.

"I have to go down there," Melly said at last.

"Yes," Halitor agreed. "We have to find food."

Melly brushed that aside. "We can't go right now. We'll have to wait."

He just looked at her, mouth hanging open.

"Wait? We can wait to eat and sleep? After a day like this?"

Melly gave him a look that reminded him of his mother, and he snapped his mouth shut. He picked up her bow and arrows.

"Yes, go hunt," she said. "I need to think."

Halitor went. Rawgool came along, foraging for the more tender parts of the pines that grew around them. Halitor, having learned a bit about hunting in the last few days, didn't wander aimlessly about looking for game. Instead, he found a clearing and waited under cover at its edge. He'd nearly fallen asleep when a rabbit hopped out into the dusky meadow. He got lucky and the arrow went home.

Glumly HalitorHa cleaned the animal—a nasty, messy job he would far rather have left to the cooks at an inn—and carried it back to a spot near where Melly still stared down at Alcedor. He built a fire, and roasted the rabbit on a spit.

Melly still hadn't moved by the time it was done, and just for a moment Halitor thought about eating it all himself. Chivalry won. He split the carcass and took half to the girl.

"Eat. And I brought water." He handed her a waterskin he'd filled at a creek a quarter mile off, when he'd stopped to wash his hands after butchering the rabbit.

"Thanks."

He sat down beside her with his dinner, and stared at the walled town. There were a lot of lights—torches moving to and fro, and lanterns hung over doors, he supposed. In his mind he could see a candle lighting the way to bed.

Stop it, he told himself. It wasn't as if they'd

be sleeping at any inns if they were down there. Not without money. He took a bite. The meat was burned on the outside and undercooked on the inside, but he was hungry, so it was good.

A long time after she finished eating, Melly sighed and stirred. "We'll have to go down tomorrow."

"We could go around," Halitor suggested. "Just like all the others villages."

There was enough moonlight that he could see her shake her head. "We have to go down."

"Why?"

"Because my Da's down there. If he's alive," she added.

"You said you thought the bandits killed him. And you said he was a merchant and was always on the road. And that you're from some village way up the valley," Halitor said, confused.

"I lied." Her tone implied it was a matter of no importance.

His head swam. How could she lie to him? "What do you mean?" What part of her story was a lie?

She didn't answer his question. "We can't go down tonight—the gates are closed and guarded at sunset. We'll want to be with the farmers going in at dawn, though." She looked around. "Where's Rawgool?"

"Asleep by the fire." Halitor looked at her. Something was happening that he couldn't understand. Something about Melly had changed and he didn't even know what. "Why dawn? Why not later? Those bandits aren't going to dare attack us right in front of the town."

"I don't want to be recognized until I know how matters stand down there."

"Whyever not?" His head was swimming again. Who would recognize the daughter of a traveling wine and cheese merchant? "How can you find out if anyone knows where your Da is, if you don't find people who know you?"

Something else bothered him. If she'd lived in this giant walled town, rather than being on the road all the time, how had the bandits captured her? There was a lot here that he didn't understand.

After a minute, Melly said, "We lived in Alcedor, but it's been a year since I was taken. I don't know if everyone will be my friend."

"I understand. Merchants travel all over, and winter where they must. So the Garans saw you as outsiders." He didn't make it a question. She might have answered if he had, and he didn't want to hear more.

Halitor had one final thought. "You get to explain to Rawgool why we're leaving him."

"Not leaving him for good. Just while we find out what's happened."

"I'm going to bed."

He didn't even stay awake to be sure she made it safely back to the fire. He just wrapped himself in his blanket, and the next thing he knew, Melly was talking softly but urgently to Rawgool.

Halitor opened his eyes. There was no sign of sunrise, but the night had that feel that said dawn was near. It was bitterly cold and he didn't want to wake up. He didn't want to stumble down the mountain in the dark, and he didn't want to go into a strange city where something he didn't understand was going on.

The *Hero's Guide* made his duty perfectly clear. What the Damsel in Distress needed, the Hero provided. Even, he had long since decided, if the Damsel was a kitchen wench and no Princess. So he sat up, put away his blanket, and put his boots back on.

Melly had finished. She reached out and patted Rawgool's massive shoulder.

"We'll leave our packs with Rawgool, Halitor. Our swords, too. I hate going unarmed, but commoners don't carry swords in Alcedor. And I'd better stay a boy. Everything look right?"

He looked her over, trying not to see too much. The hair she'd cut before leaving the Drunken Bard was still boyishly short and ragged. So were the shirt and breeches, though happily not ragged enough to show anything they shouldn't. And a week or two of near-starvation had given her an even more boyish look.

"You'll do."

"Then let's go."

He handed his pack to Rawgool, patted the giant on the shoulder, and followed the girl into the woods. To Halitor's surprise, Melly seemed to know just where she was going, and in a few minutes they came to a path that led down the slope. At least they wouldn't break their necks climbing down cliffs in the dark.

By the time they reached the valley, there was enough light to see where they were going as Melly left the path and led them across fields away from the big gates. When they reached the road she found a hiding place in the brush, and they waited.

Halitor didn't know what they were waiting for. He gave up trying to understand and just let Melly tell him what to do, and thanked Harra, Rambuta, Scarpeg and any other gods he could think of that it wasn't raining. He passed the time trying to remember more gods from the places he and Bovrell had visited.

Melly watched a number of carts and farmers trundle past toward the city before she led Halitor up onto the road and led off at a brisk walk. In a few minutes, they caught up to an old man pulling a heavy handcart. He was making slow work of it.

"Good morning, Grandfather," Melly greeted him. "Might we help you with that? If you'll share a bit of the cheese you carry, and perhaps some bread, we could pull this load right to the market for you."

Now Halitor understood. The man gave them generous portions of bread and cheese, and he ate happily while pulling the cart, which wasn't heavy. He admired Melly's cleverness.

Then they reached the gates, and Halitor realized that the food wasn't Melly's main concern, though she ate it eagerly enough. Guards stood at the gates, eying the farmers passing before them with little apparent interest. They paid even less attention to two ragged boys and an old man pulling a shabby handcart. By taking up the cart, they had made themselves invisible.

Halitor expected that once they'd safely passed the gates, Melly would abandon the old man and his cart. Instead she led off up the wide street, following the other farmers. Calling back over her shoulder to the man, who pushed from behind, she asked, "Are you for the main market, Grandfather?"

"Nay, then, lads. That un's too grand for the likes of me. I go to the small market on Marbene Street."

"That's a piece of luck," Melly whispered to Halitor, nudging them off onto a side street. "The Marbene market is close by where I wish to go. Stop gaping!" She added. "Pretend you've seen it all before! We're local lads."

Halitor pulled up his jaw and bent more to the job. He kept watching the people and houses they passed without turning his head, which was spinning with the new sights and new thoughts. He'd believed Bovrell to be sophisticated and world-wise, and thought the man had taken him everywhere. Halitor had never seen a city half so large as this.

A quarter hour's slow going through streets crowded despite the early hour brought them to the market. The old man came around the cart and showed them where to put it. He pulled another small chunk of cheese from his store and gave it to them. Melly tried to refuse, but he insisted.

"It's ye have got me here in good time, and I'll sell out today. I don't move so well as I did, and I lost me son in the Troubles. Half the day it takes me to get here, most times. By then, the best buyers are done and gone."

Halitor wondered what "troubles" he meant. Mindful of Melly's warning, he nodded his thanks and didn't ask. Copying Melly's style, he

101

said, "We were happy to help, Grandfather, and thank ye for our breakfast."

"Now we must go," Melly said. "But mayhap we can help you home again."

"If ye be goin' back out, I'd not say ye nay, though an empty cart be an easier load than full. So are ye not of the town?"

Melly seemed not to hear the question as she led Halitor into a side street.

The market had filled his senses with colors and smells and sounds in dizzying profusion. Up the small street, the houses reverted to grey and the market noises faded. Smells grew stronger, however, and less pleasant. His nose twitched at piles of slop in the street, but Melly forged on without paying any heed. She turned up an even smaller street, then an alley.

Melly walked down the alley and stopped before a door near the end. Looking around, she drew a deep breath, as though gathering courage for whatever she expected to find inside. Raising a fist, she knocked a brisk rata-tat-tat-tat on the weathered and peeling door. Then she repeated her knock.

The door opened just enough to let Melly step inside, pulling Halitor after her. She swung it closed before turning to face the occupants. They all stood in the main living space, a room which served as kitchen and sitting room alike. In that, it was just like the house in which Halitor grew up, and all the others in their small village.

The occupants, too, seemed unremarkable. A man and a woman, older than they were young, stared at Melly in open-mounted astonishment, and then sank to their knees. The woman began to speak. Melly cut her off.

"Not now. Not yet, Charene. Get up. Yes, it's me, Melly, come back and hoping you've word of my Da."

Halitor saw the two exchange looks, then turn to consider him.

"I'm forgetting my manners," Melly said. "Halitor, this is Charene and Tiron. They are old friends of my Da. This is Halitor. He's been helping me find my way back, even though I'm a kitchen wench and no Princess. Halitor," she explained, "is training to be a Hero, and you know how they are."

"Was training," Halitor muttered. Then, remembering his own manners, he bowed and offered a hand to Charene, then Tiron. "Pleased to meet you."

Melly hurried on, as though unable to contain herself. "Bandits took me last year, as I think you know. Now I must know—did my Da escape? Or did they slay him, as I fear they must have? If he lives, I know he would come to you!"

The older couple exchanged looks that Halitor could not read. "I am sorry I was not there to defend him," Tiron said, bowing his head. Halitor didn't think that was an answer, but Melly flinched.

"He has not come to us, dearie," Charene said.

Melly turned away as though from a blow, and the woman hastened to add, "We have reason to think he lives."

Halitor looked from the old woman to the young and back, as Melly turned again and gazed into the other's face. Charene clasped

103

Melly's hand and murmured, "There's still hope, my dear. And we are not alone." Slowly, almost despite himself, Halitor began to piece together the things that had puzzled him, and understood that there was a great deal more to Melly than she'd said. He turned to see Tiron watching him, not with the rheumy eyes of old age, but with the measuring look of a warrior. The sort of warrior Halitor wished he were, even if Tiron was well past his prime.

"You're no kitchen wench!" Halitor burst out, startling all of them, including himself. "You lied to me! All this way, disdaining Princesses and playing up your low birth, and it was all lies!"

Tiron raised a hand. "Not so loud. The walls have ears."

Halitor hardly noticed him. His attention was on Melly, who sighed and looked down.

"You have to tell him," Charene advised.

"It will take such a long time," Melly complained. "And I had hoped to avoid it. It will only upset him."

"If he is to be your warrior, as Tiron was your father's, he must know," the older woman insisted. Halitor almost laughed. Him? Melly's warrior? Yet at the thought he stood a little taller.

"Very well," Melly decided abruptly. "I will tell all I know—I'm sure you two would like to hear my story as well—and then you will tell me what has happened in the city this past year." She turned to Halitor. "Sit down. This will take a while. You're right. I'm no kitchen wench, at least not usually, though that is what I was when you found me. And my father is no wine merchant. My right name is Melisande, and my father is—or was—" and her voice caught just a little—"Alcion, king of Alcedor and ruler of all Garan."

So, Halitor thought. A Princess after all. He sat down hard.

"This is my story," Melly said, and settled into a chair near the fire. She began to speak in a low voice, her speech taking on a storyteller's captivating rhythms.

CHAPTER 10: MELISANDE'S STORY

"It was almost exactly a year ago that my life was upended. Until then, Da and I lived in the castle—you saw it, on the hill in the center of the town—and I never even thought about why I lived there and others down here. Da was king and things could be no other way. Oh, I wasn't completely blind. I knew I had a good life, better than most. I liked to go down into the city, disguised as a serving-girl, and wander about. Charene and Tiron helped me—he was once one of Da's guards, and saved his life, so Da gave them this house and an income. I would pretend to be their daughter, and so met the ordinary people of the kingdom. I considered it great fun, and thought little else about it.

"Then everything started to go bad. There were more raids and robberies, and Da's army couldn't seem to keep the roads safe. That was the beginning of the Troubles of which the farmer spoke, and his son was but one of many who were killed. We were constantly under attack, and it wasn't safe for me to leave the castle. People began to mutter that if the king couldn't protect them, who could?

"When matters had gotten bad enough, they got worse. I have said I was taken by bandits, and so they were, to me. They called themselves Gathrans, and laid claim to all the valleys this side of the Ice Castle, in the name of their god Gathros. They had already taken Duria and Kargor to our east, or so they said, and now they had come to claim Alcedor and Garan. Many people believed their claims and embraced them as gods-sent, though many more saw through their lies and fought them. The last remnants of peace were shattered.

"When our guards had been beaten down by ceaseless skirmishes and uprisings, the Gathrans stormed the gates early one morning, broke into the city, and soon reached the castle."

The old couple leaned closer to hear everything as Melly reached the part of the story they did not know. "I was just getting up, and for the first time in my life I regretted I kept no servants close about me. When they broke down my door, there was no one to rush to my defense save one old kinsman who slept in a room on the same hall. An uncle of Da's he was, and harmless, being half-crippled with age. But he died for me. He could scarcely lift his sword, and they cut him down, and laughed as they did it." Melly's eyes gleamed with anger and unshed tears, though her voice remained steady. "I fought with all I had. I threw my water pitcher, my books, even my chamber pot. They didn't like that. Then I took up my candlestick and tried to use it as a sword.

"They could have killed me. I thought they would, for I marked many of them, and I only wanted to kill as many as I could before they slew me, though I knew little of fighting. But they wanted me alive, and took their bruises to get me. My fury did me no good. Eventually one got behind me, and I was struck down, and swooned. I knew no more for many hours.

"When I awoke I found that I was far from home, and was now the property of bandits, or slavers. I was sick—sick from the blow, and sick with the belief that they must have killed Da as they had killed Uncle Alron. And I feared what they intended for me, during that first long night.

"Only one thing gave me hope. With no other weapons, I used everything I knew of being royal, and wrapped myself in a dignity it was hard to feel, clad as I was only in my nightgown, which had suffered much in the fight. I demanded they return me to my home and my father, and said that if they would do so at once, I would seek clemency for them. Otherwise, father's vengeance would be swift and fatal.

"Their leader, a great, coarse man they called Zarad, laughed at my threats. He told me my Da was surely dead, for though he had not yet been taken when Zarad left with me—how my heart leapt at that news!—he could neither escape nor hide from the Gathrans, and certainly was in no position to make demands. Though he hadn't meant to, Zarad gave me the hope I needed, small though it was. If Da had escaped the initial slaughter, he might yet live, and if he lived, he would find me. And Zarad had told me, too, that he was a part of the Gathran conspiracy, not just a bandit. That was both more and less hopeful, for I had no idea what they meant for me, nor why they had not killed me outright.

"That small glimpse of hope sustained me through the dreadful weeks that followed. I will not speak of that journey, when I was bound to a horse daily and beaten nightly."

Halitor made an angry noise, and Melisande paused in her telling to lay a gentle hand on his. "They did me no lasting harm," she said, and stared into the fire for a moment before resuming her tale.

"When we reached Carthor in Loria, and the inn called The Drunken Bard, Zarad was fed up with me, for I would not submit despite their cruel treatment. He declared that they had gone far enough, and I would be safe there, as slave to the innkeeper, and so I was sold.

"In that, I think he misread Derker, the innkeeper, for though a stern master and none too honest, he was never cruel, and made no attempt to break my spirit nor to force me into the kind of work I would not do. For my part, I learned to keep quiet and act like a servant, though it came hard to me. I waited several months, until they had nearly forgotten I was a slave, before I attempted to flee. I had become so trusted that they would let me go and hunt for the fresh greens that grow wild on the hills, and each time I was sent out, I went farther and stayed longer, so that the cook should get used to my long absences.

"Yet when the day came and I turned higher into the hills instead of returning, you know what happened."

Here she glanced at Charene and Tiron, and explained.

"An ogre took me, and Halitor was right: I

109

lived because I was a princess, and not a kitchen wench. Your fool of a master could not see that, Halitor. Or perhaps he didn't care, as there was no hope of a cash reward, and neither of us had any interest in the marriage which tradition would dictate occur after such a rescue. It was ordained that a Hero should be riding by at the right time to save me, but nothing could force Bovrell to be other than a glutton and a cad.

"When I found that Bovrell had abandoned his apprentice along with the bill for his lodging, I took new hope, despite what I had seen in the hills. You dropped your sword, Halitor, but at least you had one, and you wanted to be a Hero. You were neither cad nor coward. That was enough for me."

Again she paused and looked from Halitor to the old couple. When she went on, she spoke to Charene and Tiron.

"It took a long time to persuade Halitor, to undo the effects of humiliation and convince him to run with me. At last we were ready, and I had learned to use a sword, as well. Had I known a year ago what I know now, I would not have been taken so easily!"

"That might not have been a good thing for you," Tiron observed.

The girl ignored that. "So we have arrived here in Alcedor, and another ally lies up in the hills. I will have my father, and my kingdom, back!"

Melisande sat back in her chair, trembling slightly, and staring at each of them in turn.

"So tell me. Does my father yet live? Where is he?"

The older man stirred in his chair, and met her gaze. "As Charene said, we do not know. But not all in the Valley are cowed by the Gathrans, and fewer still love them. There are rumors and murmurings."

"Somewhere in the hills," Charene clarified, "someone is gathering those who would resist. Xylon and his supposed Gathrans—and I don't for a minute believe they have anything to do with any gods—are fearful, up there in your castle. And bandits range the Valley at will. So they keep the city under guard, as you saw at the gates, and punishments for ever more minor sins grow more and more severe."

"As with tyrants in all the books," Melly observed. Halitor nodded. The *Hero's Guide* had a whole chapter on tyrants: what they did, and the Hero's duty to curb their excesses.

"How have you two remained free?" he asked.

Tiron and Charene exchanged looks. "I don't think they know of us, or care," he said. "I was never a noble, only the king's guard, and now I am old. They do not concern themselves with the likes of us."

"We have been able to help a few nobles escape to the hills," Charene added. "The Gathrans care nothing for the common people. That is where our strength lies."

Melly was already saying, "Tell me what happened here, from the day I was taken. Little news came over the mountains to Loria, and I never knew what could be believed."

"It's not a pleasant tale, child," Charene warned. Halitor could have told her that

111

wouldn't stop the Princess Melisande from demanding they tell her what she wanted to know.

It seemed they knew that, for Tiron began the story without delay. "When Xylon and his followers invaded, they killed most of the guard when they took the city gates. There were so few left in fighting trim, thanks to the raids, as you well know. Xylon had planned well, curse him! He wore down the guard with small attacks and market riots, using bandits to stir up rebellion on the one hand and frighten folk on the other, until people didn't know what to believe. By the time they came in force, nearly all the commoners had lost family to the Troubles, and few had the heart to defend king or country. Then it became clear that Xylon had a witch on his side, and people grew still more fearful."

Melly stirred, and exchanged looks with Halitor. He remembered the old woman on the road, talking until he could not muster the will to stir a muscle. The same witch? Had there been more to that encounter than met the eye?

Tiron continued his story. "We only know from the reports of others what happened at the castle that day, for as you may remember, My Lady, your father had sent us over to Duria to learn what had happened there. That land did not belong to the Gathrans! They had lied.

"We arrived back after the gates had fallen, too late for our tidings to matter. There was no way to fight through to the castle, for Xylon had many men. It was by then nearly noon, and we suffered much from not knowing the fate of you or your father. The Gathrans were everywhere in the city, and fighting had for the most part ceased. We soon heard that all the guard were slain or taken, and that neither you nor your father had been seen among the living or the dead. We feared the worst."

"How did you learn I yet lived?" Melly asked.

"It was weeks later. We found a few loyal Alcedorians, and together we worked to learn all we could. Some labored in the castle, and one maid was able to report much that we could otherwise never have known. She was the first to tell us that Alcion had never been taken, and none knew where he was.

"One day an ugly brute of a man came to the castle, one dressed as a bandit and received as a friend. He met with Xylon in private conclave. Our friend knows all the secrets ways through the castle, and was able to listen in secret. We learned then that you had been taken and sold as a slave in a far land, though he did not say where—Xylon stopped him, saying he had no wish to know, as long as you never came back."

"Zarad," Melly spat out the name.

Charene nodded. "So it would seem. Our friend wept as she reported how the two men had laughed, and Zarad assured the other you would never escape. They called each other 'brother' and she believes that they are, indeed, kinsmen, for she never saw two more alike in face or spirit."

"I thought the man was more than just a bandit," Melly murmured. "And he is about again." She looked at Halitor in apology. "I did not want to say so, but it was Zarad who led the bandits who took us at the witch's hut. I do not

113

know if he saw through my disguise. Though I am much changed, Charene knew me at once."

"I have known you since you were born," Charene said. "I know you as a mother would, no matter how you are changed. I doubt Zarad would have seen the princess in the ragamuffin boy."

"After taking the castle," Tiron resumed the tale, "Xylon and about forty of his men settled in and, as we have said, began making and enforcing ever more laws. After a month or two, as they relaxed and grew confident, we began to create small disruptions. It was then that I became aware that our small group within the city walls was not the only group of loyalists, for strange things began to happen all up the Valley."

"Strange things?" Melly repeated.

"Supplies vanished between farm and castle, laborers walked away from their work, and Gathran soldiers vanished from their posts, never to be seen again, alive or dead. Finally, a week ago, we received a message."

"A message?" Melly turned from the fire to fix him with a sharp gaze.

"Nothing written, of course. The message passed from one loyal farmer to another, until it was whispered to Charene in the market, and the gods only know what may have been lost or changed, with so many repetitions."

"The message?" Melly demanded.

Charene spoke up. "It was only this: 'Our old enemy is back, and it is she who controls the Usurper.'"

Melly sat back, with a look almost of satisfaction as if, Halitor thought, some idea of hers had been confirmed. He felt no such satisfaction, having no idea what was meant.

"Who is the old enemy?"

Melly turned and looked at Halitor, almost as if she had forgotten his presence.

"Grandmother," she said flatly.

Confused, Halitor remembered the witch, and Melly's respectful form of address. She couldn't mean that! "You don't mean the old woman? The witch?"

She nodded.

"But 'grandmother' is just the polite way to address an older woman, is it not?"

She nodded again, then shook her head. "Maybe not, in this case. I mean yes, that was what I meant at the time, but even then I had my suspicions."

"You didn't know her then! And she didn't know you."

"Did she not?" Melly challenged. "What could better explain her pursuit of a pair of starving boys? And I already knew the bandit leader was Zarad, though thanks be to all the gods, he did not seem to know me. If Grandmother was behind the coup, would you want to wager she wasn't also behind my kidnapping?"

Put that way, Halitor couldn't deny it sounded likely. "Could she have known we were coming? How did she happen to be there when we needed food?"

"I don't know. Perhaps she had word of my escape. Perhaps it was just miserable bad luck." She thought a moment in silence. "This changes things. Or does it?" For the first time since

Halitor met her, Melly seemed uncertain.

Halitor still struggled to wrap his mind around what she had said. "Your grandmother plotted to overthrow her own son?"

"No, silly. She was Ma's mother. She never did like Da. Nor Ma, either. I mean, Grandmother didn't like Ma. And of course she hated me."

"Why?" Halitor couldn't imagine it. His own mother wasn't too keen on him, but she had good reason. He didn't think Melly's Ma could have been clumsy and useless and good for nothing, the way he was. And who could hate Melly, who was pretty and clever and good at everything?

"Ma was supposed to have been a boy and gone and got a kingdom for her. For Grandmother, I mean. Marrying a king wasn't as good, though it might have done if Ma hadn't died giving birth to another useless girl. Then Da threw Grandmother out of Garan for using her witchcraft to cheat people. It seems she didn't take that well, and somewhere she found men willing to do her bidding."

That did make the situation clearer to Halitor.

"Oh." He thought a moment, and changed the subject. "So we should go find your Da now, right?"

Melly frowned some more, looking from one to another of them. "That's what I don't know."

Thus began many hours of debate and discussion.

It was near dark when they left the old farmer's cart in his yard and disappeared into the woods once again, and Halitor could relax for the first time in hours. Their ploy to enter the city that morning had seemed to him a lark. Getting back out undetected he now knew to be a matter of life and death. It made it a great deal harder.

They had talked so long with Charene and Tiron, deciding what might be best to do, that Halitor and Melly had nearly missed the farmer. They'd caught him only a block from the gate, and taken some chaff for enjoying the town too much to remember their work.

That fit so well with their disguise that Halitor gave the farmer a sharp look. He appeared as stolid and dull as could be. Maybe he hoped to convince them they worked for him now. But he winked at Melly just as they parted, and made no effort to detain them.

Halitor thought about that for a long time, as they climbed the hill in the growing dusk. Finally he spoke.

"Melly," he began, then stopped. "I suppose I should say Melisande now. Or Princess Melisande?" he added dubiously, with a look at her boy-cut hair and breeches.

She made an impatient gesture. "Forget it. It's safer not to say that name aloud, and anyway, I like Melly much better. And you'll get all nervous and awkward if you have to think about me being Princess Melisande."

"Fine." He breathed a sigh of relief. He didn't think he could roam the wilds with Princess Melisande the way he could with Melly the kitchen wench. "So, do you think that farmer suspected something?"

117

"Of course."

"What if he tells?" Halitor felt for his sword, which he wasn't wearing, and looked back to be sure they weren't followed.

"Don't be silly. When he told us his son was killed, he was telling us he's on our side."

Halitor thought that sounded like an awful lot to read from a few words. It was Melly's home, though, and she was in charge.

It was dark when at last they neared their camp, and now Halitor understood that Melly knew these hills inside out, and had not happened on the spot by chance.

Not even a faint glow of coals guided them to the camp. That wasn't right. Could Rawgool have fallen asleep and let the fire die? Something was wrong; Halitor could feel it.

Melly had already entered the clearing and could see what was wrong.

Their camp was gone.

CHAPTER 11: HALITOR THE SCARED

Gone? How could the camp be gone? They must have come to the wrong clearing! Halitor's mind scrambled for answers while he scrambled about seeking clues in the dark. He found their fire pit and stooped to feel the coals. There was only the faintest hint of warmth. It had been out for some hours.

No other sign of their camp remained. Their packs—and their weapons—were gone with Rawgool.

"Rawgool could have taken it all and found a better hiding place," Halitor offered. "Maybe he heard someone coming."

Melly frowned. "There's no sign of a struggle, and it would be a struggle for anyone to take Rawgool. Except maybe his Ma. I don't know. Would he think of hiding, and taking our gear?"

"He might, I guess. He's not keen on fighting. And it would be like him to hide, and leave the fire burning as a beacon."

"True." Melly studied the clearing some more, as though hoping for an answer from the crushed grasses and scuffed dirt.

"What do we do? Even if he's safe we can't find him in the dark."

"No. We'll have to wait until morning. Anyway, I'm too tired for anything but—oh, curse it!"

"What?!" Halitor whirled about to face whatever was sneaking up behind him.

"He's taken our blankets."

Halitor looked around blankly. It was true. They would have to get through the night with nothing but the clothes they wore, though perhaps he could light the fire again. He crouched by the cold ashes, and looked up on hearing an odd sound. Melly sat on a log nearby, her face in her hands, and her shoulders shook.

Was she crying? Halitor couldn't believe it. And what was he to do if she was? He concentrated on his flint and steel and hoped he would not have to comfort a crying female. That had always been Bovrell's job.

Eventually Halitor produced a spark, and when he'd nursed it into a flame he said, "At least we can sit close to the fire and stay warm." Melly looked up, and moved closer. It was too dark to see if there were any traces of tears, and to his immense relief her voice was steady when she spoke.

"Thanks, Halitor. Let's get some leaves and branches to lie on." Halitor heaved a sigh of relief. He must have imagined her sobs. Melly had been through too much to cry over a cold camp.

Thanks to the cold night without blankets, they had no trouble rising at the first hint of daylight. They'd shivered through the night, huddled together for warmth and not sleeping much, while Halitor fed bits of wood into the small fire that warmed them only in places. The continued absence of rain should have been a consolation, but they were too cold to appreciate how much colder they could have been.

At least they had a bit of bread for breakfast, since the farmer had given them another loaf when they returned the cart to his farm. Halitor and Melly huddled by their fire and munched while waiting for enough light to track Rawgool. However or why ever he'd gone, it would be hard for him not to leave a trail a child could follow. They would find him.

So it was. When there was enough light, they could clearly see a trail leading up the mountain, with Rawgool's large prints intermixed with those of other booted feet.

Melly stood looking at the tracks, then shrugged. "Whatever else we do, we have to go after him. He's our responsibility. Let's go."

Halitor started to follow, then stopped her. "Whoever took him, they'll know by our packs he wasn't alone. Won't they leave a guard, or watch the trail or something?"

"They did."

The two turned at the words, slowly, so as not to startle anyone. The voice sounded like the kind of voice that might not like them to make sudden moves.

Halitor breathed a small sigh of relief when he'd turned. Whoever the man was, he was not one of the bandits they'd already escaped once. That had to be good. On the other hand, the eyes under a fringe of badly-cut dark hair looked hard and cold, and there was no sign that their captor and Melly recognized each other, as he would expect if this was one of her father's men. Into whose hands had they fallen now?

"Your large friend isn't very bright," the man said.

"He's not stupid," Melly said, but not as though she really meant it.

"We surrounded him and said we had his friends, and he came right along."

Of course. It would never occur to Rawgool that someone was lying, because he didn't lie. Halitor was pretty sure the giant didn't know how.

"Not knowing how to lie doesn't make him stupid." Halitor found himself defending his friend.

"Close enough. Move."

Since the dark man had a spear and sword, and they had no weapons but their belt knives, Halitor and Melly moved where he pointed, up the giant's trail.

They soon rejoined the main trail up the mountain, and their captor pointed his spear to indicate they should climb. That had to be good. Xylon's Gathrans would take them down to the town, right? Who lived up on the mountain? Halitor felt his heart pound. If he'd understood what he'd been told the day before, the Alcedorian loyalists lived up there.

And bandits, insisted the part of him that had learned a lot since Bovrell abandoned him. Sneaking another look at the grim-faced man who prodded them onwards, Halitor had a nasty feeling that the man was more likely a bandit than a noble. Just because he wasn't one of the bandits they'd already met didn't mean he was a nice person. After that, Halitor concentrated on climbing—and on staying between Melly and the spear, as the *Hero's Guide* would insist he should.

After an hour's climb through the increasingly warm morning, Halitor had sweat dripping from his pug nose, and even Melly seemed to be a bit damp about the back of the neck, Princess or no. So much for the Guide and its advice on Princesses! He began to wonder if the book had gotten anything right. When their captor ordered them to halt, Halitor was only too glad to stop moving his feet. He raised his head to look around. They didn't appear to be much of anywhere. Was this where they'd be killed and robbed? The thought almost made him laugh, since robbing them would be a huge waste of time. Anyway, the bandits or whatever they were already had anything of value he and Melly owned, since they'd taken Rawgool, the packs, and their swords.

While Halitor thought about this, men began stepping out from the brush to surround them, and Halitor prepared himself, yet again, to die in defense of the Fair Maiden. He laid a hand on his belt knife, which their captor hadn't bothered to take.

Then he felt Melly relax next to him, and turned—and saw her smile.

Halitor let out the breath he hadn't known he was holding. Perhaps he wouldn't have to die today. A moment passed with no one speaking, and he felt less sure. The spears that the rough collection of men had leveled at them didn't waver. No one greeted Melly with either the joy or the respect he would expect of loyalists encountering the daughter of their leader.

Melly's smile faded. "Sarnan? Kellan?" She looked from one man to the other. "Don't you know me?"

"No." The single word fell like a stone into the silence following Melly's question.

The girl drew herself up, and in that moment Halitor could see her clothed in the raiment of a noble, and she spoke in a voice that was no stranger to command. "Am I truly so much changed? I am the Lady Melisande da Garan, daughter of Alcion da Garan, and your sovereign ruler." She might have said more, but a guffaw interrupted her, and an older, more thoughtful-looking man spoke up.

"Nice try, lad. But our Lady was taken away and is probably dead, and she's not one you'd take for a lad." The one she'd addressed as Sarnan spoke with less confidence in his tone than in his words. He and several others peered uncertainly at the ragged boy with a regal bearing, who looked down her nose at them, as much as a girl could look down her nose at persons several inches taller than she.

"This one's no prince anyway," a stocky, hard-looking man stated, prodding Halitor with his spear. "A spy if ever I saw one."

Fear never did make Halitor sensible. He turned on the man, knocking the spear aside. It was replaced with half a dozen others, which he ignored. "No. I'm not a prince. Nor am I any spy. I am a Hero."

His face turned redder than ever as the men burst out laughing.

"Don't you think you're a bit on the young and skinny side for a Hero?" the one called Sarnan asked, not unkindly, though he made no effort to hide his amusement. For Halitor, this was the all-too-familiar litany of failure, and he turned red, and could find no words.

Not so Melly. "Halitor may be young and only an apprentice Hero, but he has saved my life more than once on our journey from Loria. Which, I might add, is where those Gathran scum sold me as a slave to an innkeeper. I was neither killed nor degraded as Zarad must have hoped, and with Halitor's help I escaped to reach my home."

Her defense of him freed Halitor's tongue, even as he turned redder. "And Melly is a girl, and a Princess, even if she is good at disguising herself as a boy. She cut her hair and took boy's clothes to be safer on the road. But what does that do if it only makes her own people want to kill us because they can't recognize their own Princess?"

The men smiled, and tried to hide their smiles, which made them seem less frightening even if it did prove they didn't take Halitor and Melly seriously. Sarnan and Kellan, however, looked a great deal less sure of themselves as Melly and Halitor spoke.

Melly followed up the advantage. "Charene and Tiron knew me right enough. Of course, she has the clear Sight."

Sarnan, who seemed to be the leader, leaned on his spear. "I think we need to go sit down and talk this over." To a murmur of protest from his men he snapped, "If they are not who they say they are, I scarcely think a pair of skinny boys pose a serious threat to twenty armed men!"

Even Halitor and Melly had to concede the truth of that. They followed Sarnan to the rebels' camp, though they had little choice in any case.

Things began looking up when they reached the camp. Not only was there hot tea and food, but Rawgool leaned against a rock, sound asleep and guarded by two heavily armed men. Halitor and Melly would have rushed to him at once, but Kellan stopped them. "Let him sleep. He fretted so over you two, we had to drug him. He'll wake up in an hour or so and be fine." Kellan looked more intently at Melly and shook his head. "'Melly.' That's what he called you, too. It did seem an odd name for a boy."

"I didn't want to use my real name," Melly said. "It would have led to trouble in Loria, and would have scared Halitor to death. I'm sorry, Halitor," she added as he opened his mouth to protest. "You know it would have."

He shut his mouth. She was right, it would have. It did.

It took an hour's talk, but in the end the men accepted that Melly was the Princess Melisande. As she sat among them and spoke, Melly's voice and bearing gradually become more those of a princess, or at least a noble, and less those of either the lad or the kitchen wench she'd pretended to be. Halitor watched in fascination as Melly faded and Melisande emerged ever more clearly in his mind—and, more importantly, in the minds of their captors.

The story Melly told of her adventures gave Halitor more credit than he thought his due, making him sound something of a Hero, just as she had done when telling their tale to Charene and Tiron. He wondered if that was part of being a Princess: making people feel good, and giving others the credit for your own triumphs. The *Hero's Guide* wasn't real big on humility. Halitor couldn't take time to sort all this out, however, for Rawgool showed signs of awakening.

Lest he awaken frightened or angry, either of which could be hazardous to himself and others, Halitor and Melly went to the giant at once, patting him on his massive shoulders and reassuring him that all was well. At last he opened his eyes and focused on Melly.

"I'm sorry, Melly. I'm not a very good guard." He looked so woebegone that Halitor almost laughed. Instead, he joined Melly in assuring Rawgool that no harm was done.

Sarnan approached, and shook the giant's hand.

"I apologize for your treatment, Rawgool, and thank you for your assistance to the Princess Melisande."

"Princess?" Rawgool looked from Sarnan to Melly and back. "Are you a Princess, Melly?"

She nodded. "I'm afraid so."

A range of emotions warred for space on Rawgool's face, until laughter won.

"What's the joke?" Kellan asked.

"Princess. Princess. I'm a giant. Ma'd say I should keep a princess hostage, or eat her or something. It's in all the stories, she says.

127

Instead, I go and help her!" He sobered. "I don't think I'd better go back to Ma."

Sarnan studied the giant, then nodded once, as though understanding something that had puzzled him. "I must admit, the presence of a giant in your camp made it hard to believe you were who you claimed to be, Princess Melisande. I see now that Rawgool," and he bowed to the giant, "is no ordinary giant."

"A new and improved sort, I should say," Melly agreed. Rawgool, who had begun to look glum again at the thought of his Ma, broke into a broad grin.

"Can I go and find some trees now?" he asked. "I'm hungry."

"Trees?" The men were understandably puzzled.

"Rawgool is a vegetarian giant," Melly explained. "He eats trees. Or parts of them, anyway."

"And broccoli," Rawgool reminded her. "Cabbage gives me gas."

This revelation left the men speechless, and Sarnan waved the giant off. "Go eat," he managed after a moment.

Rawgool hesitated, his huge brown eyes on Melly. She nodded. "Go on. We'll be fine here. All is well, Rawgool."b The giant, completely trusting, lumbered off.

Melly turned back to the rebel leaders. "Very well. I want to go to my Da. He'll be worried about me, and we need to—" She broke off as Sarnan shook his head.

"That won't be possible, my lady."

"What do you mean?" She might have

snapped the question imperiously, but to Halitor it sounded more like she asked it in desperate fear of the answer. For himself, Halitor just wanted to know something, anything, for sure. He'd never really known what was going on since meeting Melly. It would be nice to understand for once.

Sarnan nodded, unsmiling. "He is well, my lady, as far as I know," he said, addressing Melly's fear. He did less for their need for information. "Our plans to retake Alcedor are already in motion, and at this point we cannot go to him. For safety, his group will remain apart from ours, and we are not to know exactly where they are. Thus if we fail, he may remain free to try again."

"And the other way around?"

Sarnan shifted and didn't look at her. "Well, my lady, it is possible."

Even Halitor could read his meaning: possible, but not likely. Sarnan's group had the more dangerous job, and for once Halitor understood something before Melly did, so that he already knew what would come of Melly's next question.

"So what are we doing? And do we start soon?"

"We will move in tonight," Sarnan said with significant emphasis. "You will stay here with your two unusual but apparently effective guards."

Melly said a word that Halitor had learned from his first apprentice master and which he was pretty sure Princesses weren't supposed to know. There were gasps from some of the men, while others hid smiles behind raised hands. Sarnan looked disapproving.

"I'll not wait here like some...some helpless girl while you go win my kingdom back for me!" Melly snapped.

"Your father would have my head, and rightly so, if I took you with me and something happened to you, my lady." All the men nodded in agreement and alarm.

Melly drew a breath to argue, looked again at the men, and subsided. "You are right. I'll stay here."

Halitor couldn't believe his ears. Melly giving in without a fight? She was up to something. Sarnan didn't know her as well as Halitor did, he decided. The rebel leader nodded and appeared satisfied.

"May I know what the plan is?" Melly asked, all calm reasonableness.

Sarnan shook his head, but before he could refuse outright, Kellan broke in.

"I see no harm in it. It would seem she has some right to know."

Sarnan frowned, scowled, and gave way to some inner struggle, before nodding. "In short: we go down, enter the town with the help of confederates at the rear gate, and mount a frontal assault on the castle just before dawn."

"And Da and his men?"

"Only I know what they will do, so if anyone is taken he cannot be betrayed."

"Oh." Melly sank into thought, and remained there so long that Sarnan said, "If my lady is satisfied, we must rest. We will be marching and fighting all night."

Melly went on sitting and thinking as the men settled themselves in shady spots to nap. She sat so long that Halitor, too, fell asleep, as he had not done the previous chilly night.

A gentle shake woke him, and a hand over his mouth prevented him speaking. A few blinks to clear the sleep from his eyes, and he could see that it was Melly. She gestured for him to follow her away from the camp. Rawgool had returned and was asleep again.

Once safely away from the others, Melly sat down on a log. Halitor squatted beside her.

"I'm not staying here while others fight for me!" Melly kept her voice low, but no less impassioned for that.

Halitor nodded. "I know."

That disrupted the rant and the explanation she'd been about to launch. "You do?"

"Of course. And," he added, "I should argue with you, but I won't. I don't want to be left behind either."

"Good! I knew you were a Hero for real."

Halitor turned pink and his ears got hot. "What are we going to do?" he asked to distract himself from her compliments.

"I have that all figured out," Melly said.

I knew that, Halitor thought, but thought it was better not to say, as she launched into a low-voiced account of her plan.

CHAPTER 12—HALITOR THE DESPERATE

The little band of rebels had left them long since, and darkness covered the mountain. The clouds had gathered once more, and though no rain fell as yet, the night was dark and brooding. The three left behind waited, drawn close to their fire. Melly had told Halitor the general outline of her plan, but she wouldn't say anything about details. He gave up asking.

Rawgool had put up some fuss about not going with the soldiers, but when he realized that Melly and Halitor weren't going either, he calmed down. All he wanted was to stay with Melly. Protecting her was what he had promised to do, and he would do it. For him, it was that simple. There being no immediate threat, he went to sleep again.

Halitor looked at him, fought back a wave of envy for his easy rest, and nudged Melly. "Is that what all giants do? Sleep any time there's nothing better to do?" He was too edgy for sleep.

Melly wasn't interested. "Probably."

Halitor could tell by her face that she was plotting again, so he occupied himself with thinking about Rawgool and wondering whether he was like other giants at all. As Halitor didn't know any other giants—not personally—he didn't make much progress on that line of thought. The *Hero's Guide* said that giants were "capable of thought, though not what you'd call intelligent." Rawgool wasn't bright in a human way, but he had his own kind of smarts. Halitor wondered again if the Guide had much of anything right. The section on Princesses didn't seem to apply to Melly, and the dragon hadn't eaten them. And the Guide insisted that giants also ate people, but Rawgool said that even his Ma hadn't ever actually done so, except once by accident. Well, maybe the Guide was right about ogres. They seemed to be at least as nasty as the book suggested.

Before Halitor could tie himself completely in mental knots, Melly stirred from her thoughts and touched Rawgool on the shoulder. "Time to wake up."

Obediently, Halitor and Rawgool rose and followed her through the woods to the trail. How she knew where she was going mystified Halitor, who couldn't see a thing. Descending the trail was harder than the previous night. There was no moonlight at all, and the upper trail was rough and rocky, so that they stumbled a great deal. They couldn't see where they were putting their feet, or even if they were still on the trail.

In the end, Melly had Rawgool go first. He seemed able see in the dark, and neither stumbled nor slipped. Nor did he hesitate about which way to go. With Rawgool in front of them, when Melly slipped she fell against Halitor, and he slid into Rawgool. No one rolled down the mountain, to Halitor's relief. They were cold, even shivering a bit, when they started. The effort of climbing down the mountain in the dark soon warmed them.

Halitor found himself envying the giant. Until now, Rawgool had offered Halitor some dim comfort that, however dull-witted he himself might be (and Halitor's mother had made sure he and everyone else knew he was both slow and clumsy), it could have been worse. He could have been as stupid as a giant. Now, Halitor had to admit that Rawgool had compensations for his simple thought-processes, while he, Halitor, seemed stuck with his own failings. As he slid into the giant for the tenth time, he wondered if he would be any use to Melly at all. Maybe he should have stayed back in camp.

This depressed musing did at least serve to distract him from the discomfort of their stumbling and sliding descent. And the trip itself, with all its hazards, served to distract him from what might come at the end of it.

A long time later, the ground flattened out, and Melly hissed, "Wait. I have to find the way." She squeezed past her companions and took the lead. Halitor began to shiver again while she searched for her way, but soon he was stumbling across a pasture in her wake. There was just enough light to keep Melly and the giant in sight, and not enough to see where he stepped. He cringed as his foot sank into something soft. Someone pastured cattle in the field. The wind had picked up and cut right through the ragged garments he wore, but hurrying after the others he was soon sweating once more.

After an eternity, Halitor could just make out the city ahead of them. The clouds thinned enough to let a little moonlight through. They were circling the walls, moving around to the up-valley side, the side closest to where the castle stood on its hillock. Were they going to follow the others in through that postern gate Sarnan had mentioned? That seemed idiotic. If they went in first, they'd be killed for sure. If they went after the others, the enemy would be alert and they'd just as certainly be killed.

Melly led them unhesitatingly to a thick hedgerow a long stone's throw from the wall. For all Halitor could see, it was an impenetrable mass of thorns, but she seemed confident that there was a way through.

Melly stopped and turned to look at Rawgool, one hand going to her mouth.

"Rawgool," she whispered. "I don't know if you can come with us. I forgot—how big you are and how small the passage is. Perhaps..." Her voice trailed off, for the first time reflecting some uncertainty.

"Not go?" Rawgool sounded as though he couldn't even understand the words. "Where you go, I go."

"If you can't fit, you can't fit!" Melly protested.

"I'll fit. You'll see."

Halitor wondered how he could be so sure. Could the giant shrink himself? Or was he just stubborn? Maybe he figured if the hole was too small, he would make the hole bigger.

Melly sounded resigned. "Very well. I lead,

135

and Halitor after me, and you come along if and as you can."

And, Halitor thought, if Rawgool got stuck, they could go on.

Not that he particularly wanted to go on without the giant. There was a sort of comfort in that massive presence and single-minded determination.

Melly bent double, ducked under a thorn branch, and disappeared into what Halitor would have sworn was a solid wall of brambles. He ducked in after her, and found that the way was clear, though he had to stoop. Behind him, Rawgool made less noise than expected, given he had to crawl, pushing back the brambles on all sides. Halitor glanced back, but could see nothing in the darkness. It sounded like the giant was keeping up.

"Is this the way you think your Da is going in?" he whispered to Melly.

"No. There's another way that will take him right to the Great Hall. I want to get there first, by a different route." She paused in a small clearing and groped about in the dark. She tugged on something Halitor couldn't see, and he felt a puff of dank air, smelling of unseen underground spaces.

"We'll have to crawl for a while. Rawgool, this is where you might not fit. I'm sure you'll have to slide on your belly. Can you?"

"Yes." The giant sounded calm, and not at all out of breath. Halitor's breath came fast, and his heart pounded, though not from exertion. A tight, dark passage with armed men at the other end scared him. He'd admit that to himself, if to no one else.

"Let's go," Melly said. "Rawgool, close the hatch behind you if you can." Her voice shook just enough for Halitor to hear it. He took a deep breath, and followed her into the hole.

Halitor's first reaction was relief at being out of the wind. It was warmer underground. He could hear Rawgool creeping in behind them, and the giant's breath began to get ragged as he labored to pull himself along in the tight space. The passage was rough, and sloped downward, and it hurt Halitor's knees. He hated to think how it must feel to the giant slithering along on his belly, even with his tough hide. The unmistakable smell of cow pasture followed them too, and Halitor knew he'd been right about what he'd stepped in crossing the field.

Once Halitor bumped his head on a low spot, and he thought for sure the giant would get stuck there. With a mighty heave and a few grunts that caused Melly to shush him from the front, Rawgool forced his way past the narrow point.

Halitor's mind had begun to fill the darkness with all sorts of things he didn't want to meet, before Melly finally stopped, as he found a moment too late. He took his hand off her foot and waited while she stood up. A moment later, a hand reached down, touched his head, and fumbled along his arm to his hand. She pulled him to his feet. Rawgool lay still on his belly, with no room to move ahead.

"Be extra quiet now." Melly's voice was barely a wisp of sound. "We're under the Great Hall."

The passage was not only larger here, but the floor was smoother, and sloped. Halitor moved up the slope with Melly, and Rawgool was able to wriggle out of the hole and onto hands and knees. He still couldn't stand, but at least he could crawl, and kept up easily as they moved cautiously along the passage.

Halitor's sword scraped on the stones, and Melly hushed him urgently. After that, he kept it clutched to his chest, where it couldn't touch the walls.

He could feel the weight of the hill and the castle pressing down on him in the dark. He started to sweat. They were too far down! If Melly hadn't blocked him in front and the giant behind, Halitor would have broken into a run, trying to flee the darkness and that sense of pressure.

Just when he knew he couldn't stand it a moment longer, the passage changed. Melly pulled him by the hand, and he could feel her moving upward more steeply, tugging him after her. His foot touched a step. That broke his panic, and he distracted himself further by thinking how uncomfortable it all must be for Rawgool, who now climbed the rough stone stairs on all fours.

By the time they stopped Halitor was again near to screaming, from the tension and the darkness and the sense of walls closing in. He had never known that he didn't like small dark spaces, not having been in any. Now he swore he would never enter one again.

Melly moved, and light struck his eyes painfully, accustomed as they were to the utter darkness. In a moment his eyes adjusted and he realized it was only a tiny, dim speck. Melly spoke in his ear, and though her voice was so light as to be a mere breath, it still seemed to carry confidence.

"We're in the south tower. The room is empty, as I'd hoped. I'm going in."

Halitor put a hand on her shoulder.

"No. I go first." He laid his other hand on his sword, then changed his mind and drew his knife. That would be better if he had to kill a guard.

Halitor never killed anyone, nor wanted to. Except for those bandits, he reminded himself. He'd have killed them happily enough if he'd had the weapon to do it. If he'd known back at the witch's cottage what they had done to Melly, he might have tried to kill them even without weapons. And the people holding the castle were allies of those bandits. He gripped his dagger more firmly.

Melly opened the door a crack, and there was a little more light. It steadied Halitor's mind, and he peered over her shoulder into the room, which appeared to be a small dressing room. Still no one appeared, and no alarm sounded. He pushed the door open and stepped quickly through and to one side, knife at the ready.

The room was truly empty. Melly stepped out behind him. It took both of them to pull Rawgool out, still on hands and knees, and help him to the middle of the room, where he sat rubbing his legs.

The clouds had cleared still more while they were underground, and now moonlight streamed through the windows. Halitor saw that the giant had dirt and leaves in his hair and scrapes on his face, but after a moment Rawgool levered himself to his feet. His head cleared the ceiling by inches.

Melly led the way out of the little room and through a comfortable-looking but plain bedroom.

"Da's room," she whispered. "It looks like Xylon hadn't had nerve enough to move in here. I suppose the Usurper liked the Grand Suite better," she added. "Da always said that was for people who needed props to tell them they're important."

"Sh!" hissed Rawgool. Both turned to look at him in surprise. The giant had never given an order. He leaned much closer and whispered, so soft they could scarcely make it out, "Someone in the next room."

They didn't question how he knew. His giant's ears could pick up sounds they couldn't hope to hear. Halitor, his dagger again at the ready, opened the door a crack and peered through. He couldn't see anyone, but now he could hear little scuttling noises, like a small frightened animal. He stood aside so Melly could peek, and after a moment she relaxed. Then she pushed the door open wider and stepped into the room before Halitor could stop her. He clutched his knife and followed.

"Tilly!" Melly whispered. Then, a little louder, "Tilly!"

There was a squeak much like that of a mouse, and then a frightened voice said, "Oh! It sounds like my Lady, and she is dead! Oh, it can't be! Is the room haunted?" Halitor could now see a serving girl in a drab dress, clutching a cleaning cloth and staring about her.

"No ghost, you goose, it's really me," Melly said. "I'm not dead."

The girl stared. Then she dropped her dustrag and burst into tears. "Oh! My Lady! It is really you!" She cried even harder. "Now they'll find you and kill you for sure!"

"No they won't."

"At least, not if she quiets down," Halitor muttered, just loudly enough to be heard.

Tilly's hands flew to her mouth, her eyes wide. But she quieted at once.

"Now, Tilly," Melly whispered. She hadn't raised her voice through the whole thing. "What are you doing cleaning up here in the middle of the night?"

Halitor looked out the window at the moon, and guessed it to be only an hour or two before dawn. They had been two hours and more in that tunnel.

"It's the only time it is safe, My Lady," Tilly whispered. "I wanted—they won't let—I've been keeping it ready for Lord Alcion's return!" She looked around as she said it, as though expecting an attack.

Halitor wondered how this terrified bit of a girl could have managed to keep coming and working here against orders. He was pretty sure she really was just a servant girl, a lowly drudge, not another Princess in disguise. How did she get so brave?

"Well, it's good for us you are here," Melly said firmly. "You can tell me where everyone is.

141

Let's go back into the bedchamber, though. It's more private."

Halitor stopped her. Leaning close, he whispered, "I think Rawgool might be a bit much for her."

Melly nodded and smiled. "True. This will do, then." The two girls sat on a soft seat near the window. "First, where does the Usurper sleep?"

"In the Great Hall with all his men. I think they still fear attack, though no one has dared to rise in months. Or perhaps they all like to drink together. They do so every night, and fall asleep where they lie. Pigs!"

"Do they?" Melly sounded pleased. "Now, tell me of our people."

Halitor stationed himself by the door. He didn't know the people they discussed, and could add nothing. He could stand guard. After the tunnel, the thought of fighting didn't bother him as much as it had. Dying in a fight was preferable to dying in a dark hole.

Still, it felt like the consultation went on forever. Halitor's newfound courage was leaking out, dawn grew nearer, and Rawgool might tire of waiting any time.

At last Melly patted the maid on the shoulder. "You'd best get back to wherever you're supposed to be. Don't tell anyone you saw us."

"Many servants are still loyal, My Lady."

"Yes. But maybe not all who seem so are so. We'll take no chances, and when the fighting starts, they can show where they stand."

The girl nodded, curtsied, and walked to the door. Halitor opened it an inch and peered out.

"All clear." He opened the door wider to let her pass. "Luck to you."

The girl slipped out and was gone, running silently down the hall on her bare feet.

Melly had gone back to Rawgool in the bed-chamber.

"I have my plan now," she said when Halitor rejoined them.

About a mile of corridor later, they reached their destination, and Halitor began to remember how Melly's plans had a way of getting him into more trouble than he could handle. They stood—Rawgool crouched—in a servants' passage outside the Great Hall, from which a chorus of snores sounded, telling of a large number of men sleeping.

They had crept past the main doors, stopping to wedge a bar across them so they could not open. Now, Melly told him, only two ways in or out remained: the servant's door they guarded, and the secret passage up which she expected her father to come. Then they went to the servants' entrance and waited for the sounds of battle that would tell them Sarnan and Kellan were at the gates.

A dull, grey light had begun to reveal the features of the Great Hall before they heard anything. At last Rawgool raised his head to listen. A moment later the others could hear it too: fighting, somewhere outside. Within moments it grew louder, loud enough to wake the lighter sleepers in the Hall.

They heard a voice calling for light, and demanding to know what in the names of several nasty gods was going on. Halitor and Melly kept their eyes tight to the servants' peepholes, and someone must have lit a torch or stirred up the fire, because the room brightened, throwing the corners into deeper shadow.

A man in chain mail stood on the dais, shouting.

"It's him!" Melly said. "The dung-loving bit of vile scum."

Her hand went to the door, and she jerked it back. "Not yet, not yet. Wait," she told herself.

As the noise outside grew, the men in the hall began milling about, though the man on the dais stood still, his hand on his sword hilt. His mail gleamed in the torchlight. Halitor touched his own cotton shirt. Bovrell the Bold had worn chain mail, but his former apprentice didn't even own a leather jerkin.

"The rabble have risen," Xylon called over the noise his men made. "The peasants are revolting. No doubt the guards can handle it, but let us go and join the fun."

He spoke confidently, but his men, roused from a drunken sleep, gaped in confusion. Many tried to lie back down, to be kicked into action by their companions. As the men finally moved toward the great double doors, Melly opened the small side door and the three slipped inside. Rawgool bumped his head on the doorway and said "ouch!" but the men made too much noise to hear. No one noticed them, because servants' entrances were made to go unnoticed, even when used by a giant.

Halitor was saying, "If you guessed wrong about your Da, Melly, we are dead!" when the crowd grew louder and more active, anxiety rising. The men leading the pack could not open the doors.

Xylon strode forward, not seeing the three in the shadows where only servants went. He knocked a few men aside to get at the big doors.

"Worthless louts." He laid a hand on the door and pushed. Nothing happened. He pushed harder. The door bowed a bit, but did not yield.

A few men began edging away, looking for another way out, or just a place to get away from Xylon. They found the servants' door. They also found two lads with swords and a giant with a club, guarding the door.

Halitor didn't know just when or where Rawgool had picked up the chunk of timber he now hefted, but it had a comfortingly weighty look, unlike his own spindly sword and dagger.

The first man to spot them yelled, and more turned. Melly raised her voice.

"Lay down your arms. We hereby reclaim this castle in the name of Lord Alcion!" Aside to Halitor, under the roar of anger and disbelief and laughter, she said, "Of course they won't yield, but we have to say it." Halitor knew. It was in the Rules, and Nobles were even more bound by Rules than Heroes were.

After that, Halitor found himself too busy to consider the wisdom of their approach.

Had both he and Melly not learned more from her sword-fighting lessons than they'd realized, they wouldn't have lasted a minute. Thanks to practice, they fought better than Bovrell would have believed possible, and Rawgool soon showed the ruffians that he, too, meant business.

145

Even so, it looked bad. Better than awful was not good enough, and the three were sorely outnumbered. Yet even as they were pushed back against the door, men began to draw away from them, and shouts arose from other parts of the Great Hall. There seemed to be increasing numbers of men attacking the Gathrans, though Halitor could not see where they came from.

He had little attention to spare for such matters in any case. Halitor found himself fighting desperately against a broad chest in chain mail. He wasn't a short boy, but he had to look far up to see into the face of Xylon, who was as huge as he'd looked on the dais. Halitor rather wished he hadn't looked. The villain just grinned as he shattered the boy's light weapon with his massive broadsword.

Halitor expected to die the next second, a feeling that had grown all too familiar since he'd taken up with Melly. But Xylon didn't bother to kill him, turning instead to attack Melly. She had a better sword than Halitor, but being herself much smaller and lighter, she wouldn't stand a chance.

Desperate, Halitor looked about for a weapon. No sword or mace presented itself, as the *Hero's Guide* suggested it should in time of need. For some reason a row of wooden buckets stood near the wall. They looked heavy enough to do some damage. Hastily, he snatched one up, braced himself, and swung at Xylon's head with all his might.

That was when Halitor found out what buckets were doing in the Hall.

CHAPTER 13: HALITOR THE HERO!

The huge villain let out an outraged roar as the bucket struck him. It cut his scalp open from his ear to the top of his head, and worse, it showered him with its contents. Men who drink half the night, Halitor realized as he dropped that bucket and grabbed the next, fill a lot of slop-pots. This time he didn't try to hit Xylon, just flung the contents in the man's face.

Melly took care of the rest. Blinded by the disgusting shower, Xylon stood no chance against the enraged girl. She knocked the sword from his hand and swept his feet from under him. She stood over him and drove the point of her sword against the man's throat.

"Yield, swine!"

Halitor snatched up Xylon's massive sword, which he could barely lift, and cleared enough space with a few wild swings to pause and bellow, "Lay down your arms or your leader dies!"

His voice squeaked a little, but that didn't seem to ruin the effect. The sounds of fighting faltered, then died, as more and more men looked and saw that it was true. Many were bright enough to realize that if Xylon fell, they were all doomed. Some might have fought on out of desperation, but most gave up in despair, or were stopped by their fellows, who knew a lost cause when they saw it.

Another voice rang out across the Hall, commanding, "Yield to the rightful King!"

Halitor spared a glance to see a handsome man with a vaguely familiar face and graying hair standing erect on the dais, which had been swept clean of the enemy. Flanked by fighters in rough dress but wielding fine weapons, the man gazed across the hall at them.

"Melisande! My child!" His astonished voice carried over the shouts of fighters on both sides. Then, in a voice that shook a little, "Holy relics of Rambuta, she has a giant at her back!"

The initial bellow got the attention of any who had not yet ceased fighting. A silence fell over the hall as all eyes turned to Melly—and Rawgool, who reacted to the attention by turning an even brighter red than Halitor could. A blushing giant is hard to ignore. Giants have so much with which to blush.

Melly looked up at her father's cry, her sword not budging from Xylon's throat. If anything, she pressed a little harder, starting a trickle of blood.

"Majesty! What would you have me do with this caitiff knave? Do I slay him on the spot?"

A path opened in the crowd, and Alcion, for it was of course he, made his way from the dais to his daughter's side. He stood looking down at his enemy, drew breath to give his orders, and choked.

"Phwaw! What a stink! Truly this man reeks of the violence and evil he has wrought." His men nodded, covering their noses.

"Well, actually," Melly said, "he reeks of the

148

slop buckets Halitor used to knock him senseless so that I could disarm him." She nodded to Halitor, who now proved that, however abashed, a human simply cannot blush as over-whelmingly as a giant.

Alcion looked at the scarlet young man, then back at his daughter. His eyebrows went up. Melly cut in before he could speak, reminding him they were in the midst of a crisis.

"Orders, Father. Do we slay him? Or perhaps turn him over to those whose families were slain under his brutal and unjust rule?"

Xylon had been nearly as red as Halitor and Rawgool, but now he turned pale, at least where he wasn't covered with blood—or worse. Alcion studied him a long moment, careful to breathe through the mouth.

"Bind him. And his men! We will try them when we have settled matters. Meanwhile, they can remain in the lowest dungeon."

A growing roar from without reminded everyone that theirs was not the only battle.

"We must go forth and put an end to this fighting," Alcion called.

Before anyone could move to obey his orders, the great doors swung inward, and Sarnan entered at the head of a crowd of soldiers and citizens. He took in the scene at a glance and sank to his knees.

"All hail the rightful Lord of Alcedor!"

In a moment everyone in the room was kneeling to Alcion save Melly, Rawgool, and Halitor. Some enemy combatants were "helped" to their knees by Alcedorian soldiers, others dropped of their own accord. Halitor desperately tried to recall what the *Hero's Guide* said his proper response should be in such situations. He wasn't Alcion's subject. Heroes were no one's subjects.

Alcion ignored the little group at his back for the moment to address Sarnan, his second in command. "I take it the city is ours once more?"

"The city, and the kingdom, Majesty. Though we may have to hunt down a few bandit bands that fled rather than fight." Sarnan looked at the three standing behind Alcion, and frowned. "Lady Melisande! What are you doing here?"

"Guarding this coward and blackguard, Lord Sarnan," Melly replied coolly. Through it all, she had kept her concentration on the important thing, which was keeping her sword at Xylon's throat.

"You were commanded to remain safe!"

"And, as you can see, I am safe. Though I wish someone would take and bind this great hunk of wasted space so I can put down my sword. My arm grows weary." Xylon shifted a little as though thinking her fatigue might let him escape. "I fear I will accidentally cut his worthless throat," she added, and he lay still. "So someone please remove this piece of trash, and clean the floor. The stink is ferocious."

"Mm, yes," Alcion murmured. "Wil, Tolen, please bind the thief and—do we take him directly to the dungeons, Lord Sarnan, or need we first display him on the ramparts so all can see he is truly defeated?"

It was nearly evening before all had been sorted and arranged, and Melly, bathed and dressed as befit a princess, told her adventures yet again to an admiring court, including her father.

"And so," she concluded, "Halitor the Hero, when his sword failed him in time of need, grasped the nearest thing to a weapon and felled our enemy."

"It was you knocked him over and put the sword to his throat," Halitor mumbled in protest.

"Oh, I know I took the final step, but had you not stunned him, Halitor—and blinded him with his own blood as he was blinded by his ambition—I would have stood no chance. That is the simple truth. I owe my life and our kingdom to Halitor."

A rumbling snore from the corner caused all to turn their heads away from the blushing Halitor. Rawgool, having eaten the better part of a pine tree, topped off with a bushel of broccoli, was asleep again. Melly considered him.

"Nor might I have survived without Rawgool at my back this last week, protecting me through all our adventures. I'm no seasoned sword-maiden, to fight off such a crowd."

"Indeed not!" exclaimed Sarnan. "And I trust you will now return to your proper studies and leave off weapons and boys' clothes." He scowled at the short hair that nothing but time could amend, though Tilly had done her best to make it look respectable, trimming up the ragged bits and putting a ribbon in it.

"Oh," Melly pressed a finger into the dimple on her chin, "I don't know about that. I believe I shall continue combat lessons, and for that I fear more sensible clothing is essential. This dress is lovely, but not really practical for such pursuits."

Halitor heard a voice from among Sarnan's men whisper, "Told you she would be trouble!"

Alcion glared at his daughter, opened his mouth, and closed it without saying a word. Halitor decided to be far away when he did speak. The battle of father and daughter would make the fight in the Great Hall seem as nothing.

In the weeks that followed, Halitor found that everyone except him had something important to do. Even Rawgool was invited along when the soldiers went out to chase bandits. Once they got over thinking he would eat them, they found him good company and excellent for scaring off all sorts of perils. When Halitor offered to go along, they made excuses.

"They think I'm no good," he griped to Melly when they were alone. They were in the practice courts, listlessly doing sword drills. No one else was there, because everyone else was keeping their sword skills sharp by going out every day to battle bandits and renegades.

"Me neither. They smile when I come to practice with them. Indulgently, like you smile at a little child who attempts an adult task." Melly sounded almost as gloomy as Halitor felt. "And it's no use even asking if I can go along on a bandit hunt."

"You're a Princess," he protested. "They have to do what you say."

"Oh, yes," she agreed. "In unimportant matters they have to jump. But they don't have to take me seriously. They think," she added without looking at him, "that I should be getting married, not learning to be a warrior. Sarnan especially, and he has charge of the army."

They sparred for a while without talking. Then Halitor asked, "What are you going to do?"

"Not sure. You?" She was panting for breath now.

Halitor didn't answer until he had disarmed her. "You know what the *Hero's Guide* says?" Both leaned on their swords and gasped with the effort of the fight.

She nodded. It was common knowledge, what Heroes and the Princesses they rescued were to do, right down to "happily ever after."

"Do you want to?" he asked.

"Do you?"

Halitor toyed with the hilt of his sword. "It doesn't seem right. I mean, if a Hero has to marry every Princess he helps, then he can only ever help one Princess. That's not the way they make it sound, but it's what it boils down to." He took a deep breath. This was the first time he'd ever spoken aloud his doubts about the Guide.

"I don't want to either. Oh," Melly added quickly, "I do like you, Halitor, ever so much, but I'm not ready to settle down and just be a Princess."

He nodded. "I like you, too, Melly. But if I married you I'd never finish learning to be a Hero."

"And they'd insist you call me 'Melisande,' not 'Melly.'"

"And I'd have to learn to be a noble. Duck Gods! If I married you, I might have to be king

153

someday!"

Melly didn't say anything. She didn't have to. They both knew that thought haunted her father, as well. Alcion liked Halitor, and was duly grateful to him for aiding his daughter. He wasn't entirely happy about the sword-fighting lessons, though he admitted they'd served her well. Yet anyone could see Alcion didn't think the boy was up to the job of being king. No one did, though everyone truly liked Halitor. They just thought he was young and hapless. Not king material.

Worse, Halitor agreed with them. Alcion's arms-master was making progress in teaching him the use of the weapons appropriate to a Hero, but the seneschal despaired of teaching him the management of property, and the dancing-master gave up after one lesson, much to Halitor's relief. A task that required both grace and a close proximity to females was doomed from the start.

Halitor and Melly did the only thing they could think of. They took their dilemma to Charene and Tiron. The old couple continued to live in their humble home in the town, declining the rooms in the castle Alcion offered in thanks for their loyalty and help.

"We prefer living in the town," Charene explained. "There's so much more we can do here, among the ordinary people. And we are used to our ways."

So going to the old warrior and his wife was not only a matter of going to the best friends Melly had, but also to those most likely to encourage them to follow their own hearts, as Halitor well knew.

They put on the ragged boys' clothes they'd worn on their journey, and crept out through a secret tunnel, which was the only way Melly could go out without half a dozen bodyguards. Out on the street, Halitor drew a deep breath, relishing his freedom right down to the soles of his feet. A glance at Melly suggested she felt the same.

"Come in, come in, Melisande, Halitor," Tiron welcomed the pair warmly when they knocked on the weathered door. Once they had greeted their old friends, and Charene had sat them down by the fire with cider and seed-cakes, Melly burst out with the whole dilemma in one breath. When she finished, Charene and Tiron looked at each other, and Halitor could have sworn they smiled.

"How old are you now, my dear?" Charene asked Melly.

"You know I'm fifteen now."

"And you, Halitor?"

"I'm not sure. I think I'm about sixteen. Ma used to lie about my age to get me apprenticeships. I sort of lost track."

Charene and Tiron exchanged looks again, and Tiron nodded. "Just as I thought. You're both too young for the rules in the Guide to apply. Why, Halitor, even seventeen is too young to be an official member of the Heroes' Guild, which is required before you can marry a princess. And princesses of less than eighteen years of age are never allowed to marry Heroes of any age."

155

"Why ever not?" demanded Melly.

"Not enough experience, my dear," Charene answered. "Not that you lack experience, after what you've been through, and with Halitor being so young himself, he's scarcely likely to take advantage of your innocence."

Halitor held his breath. If Melly took this the wrong way, it would be just like her to insist on marrying him after all, just to show she was up to the job.

Melly, it seemed, had more sense than that. She looked suspiciously at the old couple, then sighed and relaxed in relief.

"It's funny no one else knew that rule," she mused. "I must set Da's mind at rest."

"On that one point," Charene teased.

"On that one point," Melly agreed. "I shall of course continue my training with weapons. Yes, and dancing lessons too," she added, as her friends looked at her. "And continue to study the management of castles and kingdoms."

"And what of you, my son?" Tiron asked. "What will you do?"

"I believe," said Halitor, thinking it out, "I would like to spend the winter here, learning from the arms-master, but no longer troubling the seneschal or the dancing-master. In the spring," he snuck a look at Melly, who gazed into the fire with her back to him, "In the spring I would like to ride out and explore the Ice Castle and maybe even ride to the Worldtop."

"Alone?" Tiron asked.

Melly turned to see his answer.

"Alone," he said without a quaver. "As a Hero should."

156

EPILOGUE: A SPRING DAY AT CASTLE ALCEDOR

Everyone came out to the courtyard to enjoy the spring sun and to see Halitor off and wish him the best. Alcion took the young Hero aside before they went out, to ask one last time, "Are you sure? You are welcome to stay as long as you want."

"And do what, my Lord?" A winter in the castle had taught Halitor much, including how to speak more like a nobleman and less like an ignorant village boy from Duria. It had also taught him that he could not live out his life as a hanger-on at court with no fixed purpose. He was more than ready to ride out and resume his efforts to become a Hero.

"No, I have to pursue my rightful task, though I thank you for your kindness." He shook Alcion's hand, then clanked down the steps in the chain mail the armorer had made for him. He mounted his horse, a gift from Alcion.

The riding-master gave a satisfied nod. They'd spent long hours over the winter transforming Halitor from a sack of potatoes in the saddle to a horseman. Melly stepped forward to hand him his bow. That was her great triumph. When everyone else had given up, she had persisted and managed to teach Halitor to shoot, well enough at least to hunt slow-moving game. She smiled at him.

"Have a good time, Halitor. And write to me. Life is going to be a lot less fun here without you."

He didn't ask if she wanted him to stay after all. They'd had that conversation the night before. Each was settled on his or her duty: he to serve all in need as a Hero, and she to learn all she had to know to be the next ruler of Alcedor. Halitor was pretty sure he had the better bargain, though Melly seemed content with her choice.

Moved by the sudden realization that he might never see these people again, Halitor swung back down from the saddle and hugged Melly, then each member of the court in turn. Even Rawgool, who now lived up in the hills where there was more for him to eat and he could keep an eye on the border—and made the citizens less nervous—had come to see him off. The giant stepped forward and clapped Halitor on the back, then caught him with the other hand before he could topple from the impact.

"You be careful. I don't want to come rescue you in the cold mountains. Giants hate the cold."

"Did your mother teach you that?" Halitor teased.

"No. I figured it out for myself during the winter." Rawgool grinned.

Everyone laughed, and Halitor turned to the last person waiting to bid him farewell. Alcion shook his hand again, and embraced him. "May the gods go with you, son. You've no need to marry Melly to have a home here, whenever you tire of roving." When Alcion released him, Halitor hastily remounted and turned his horse before anyone could see moisture on his cheeks and think he might be crying.

Half the Court had wanted to ride along that first day, but Halitor had shaken his head and refused all company. He would begin as he meant to go on. He wasn't sure what the Guide would say about that. The book lay in the bottom of his saddlebag; he hadn't looked at it for months. It seemed to contain so many errors.

The young Hero rode alone out the castle gates, and down through the streets of the city, where many waved farewell, including Charene and Tiron. Halitor started to pull up, meaning to stop and embrace them, but the old couple faded back into the crowd when he turned, and he knew they didn't want the attention. He kept riding, and did not look back as he passed through the gates.

Once on the road, Halitor relaxed in his saddle, lifted his face toward the warm spring sun, and began to sing, "The Road is Long But Memory is Longer," a very long ballad that grew less acceptable to polite company as the verses progressed. A few birds flew off for quieter perches as he sang. No one had been able to teach Halitor to sing on key, but he knew all the words.

THE END

ABOUT THE AUTHOR

Rebecca M. Douglass has been reading and writing stories since she was old enough to hold a pencil. She has a special fondness for fantasy thanks to frequent childhood visits to Narnia and Middle Earth. Ms. Douglass uses her word-processor near San Francisco, CA, where she lives with her husband and two teenage sons, while her imagination rambles where it will, in this world and out. She is the author of the delightful *Ninja Librarian* books, as well as a picture book for outdoor families, a mystery for the parents, and her newest middle-grade fantasy, *Halitor the Hero*.

Visit Rebecca M. Douglass at
http://www.ninjalibrarian.com

Made in the USA
San Bernardino, CA
02 January 2016